DARKNESS SWALLOWED HIM.

Otis waited for his eyes to adjust, peering into the gloom, seeking the staircase. In the weak light that seemed to trickle into his vision like sap seeping from treebark, he saw no stairs. Suddenly, bewilderingly, he faced—inches away—a ragged wall of rock. He looked upward through gray air at a tower of sandstone and gravel.

The wall's surface crawled and writhed like water on glass. Pits in the rock were gaping mouths that vomited knife-edged shards aimed at his eyes, cutting his face. Through a shower of stinging dirt, he lunged upward, clawing for a fingerhold on the fringe of red roots that trailed, like shreds of flesh, between the spikes and thorns that toothed the treacherous wall. He felt the ground beneath him disappear, his feet suddenly treading on emptiness. He snagged one of the thin tendrils. He was too heavy. Ripping his hands into shredded meat, he clawed for another strand as he felt his only lifeline stretch and fray against the jagged cliff face. He dared to look down at dead trees clustered together, limbs like upstretched talons, mounted on rocks that jutted and gaped like mouths full of broken fangs. Otis looked back up at the root too weak, too slippery to hold him there.

LAST KID BOOKS
by David Benjamin

The Life and Times of the Last Kid Picked

Three's a Crowd

A Sunday Kind of Love

Almost Killed by a Train of Thought: Collected Essays

Skulduggery in the Latin Quarter

Summer of '68

Black Dragon

They Shot Kennedy

Jailbait

Bastard's Bluff

Woman Trouble

Fat Vinny's Forbidden Love

Witness to the Crucifixion

Choose Moose

Dead Shot

Bistro Nights

The Melting Grandmother and Other Short Works

Voice of the Dog

An Apartment in Paris

Benjamin's Mess

Also by David Benjamin

SUMO: A Thinking Fan's Guide to Japan's National Sport

A JIM OTIS NOVEL

UPSTAIRS

BY DAVID BENJAMIN

LAST KID BOOKS

Last Kid Books
309 W. Washington Avenue
Madison, WI 53703

First Edition
March 2026

Printed in Wisconsin, United States of America

For more information or to order books:
visit www.lastkidbooks.com

Library of Congress Control Number: 2026902664

ISBN-13: 979-8-9946390-0-9

A NOTE ON THE TYPE

This book was set in Athelas, a serif typeface designed by Veronika Burian and Jose Scaglione and intended for use in body text.[1] Released by the company TypeTogether in 2008, Burian and Scaglione described Athelas as inspired by British fine book printing.

Printed and bound by Park Printing Solutions
Verona, Wisconsin

Designed by Kristin Mitchell, Little Creek Press and Book Design
Mineral Point, Wisconsin

For Junko

CHAPTER 1

(Thursday, the 22nd of May)

"That's gotta hurt."

"What the hell's he hitting him with?"

Jim Otis had just stepped out of the town's barber shop, where Mose Irons had informed him that he was developing a bald spot. With his hair already peppered in gray, this was not welcome news.

"Gettin' a hole in your roof," Mose had said in a tone of tonsorial wisdom, "makes you re-think your future and wonder if you'll ever make love to a woman again."

"Well, I'm already making love to—" Otis had broken his sentence there, realizing that this was not the sort of personal information that Carol, the woman in question, would want bandied about the barber shop—even though no one was present but Mose and him.

"It's a willow switch," said Mose.

The scene they were observing, from across Main Street, involved two boys, one cowering under an onslaught by the other, who was flogging him with what appeared to Otis to be a thin whip.

"What's a willow switch?"

Mose's smile conveyed a hint of nostalgia.

"We used to have regular battle royals with those things,"

he said. "You need a weeping willow, best in the springtime, with all those spidery branches droopin' down, touchin' the ground. You cut one off about three feet long, strip away the leaves."

"And that's a willow switch?"

"That's a willow switch. On bare skin, you can leave a nasty welt. Stings for hours."

Across the street, the willow-switch attacker had driven the slightly smaller boy into a defensive crouch in the gutter between two parked cars.

"Y'know, Chief," said Mose, invoking Otis' rank. "You might oughta do somethin'."

Otis sighed. "I oughta. Yes." He stepped off the curb gingerly, leaning on a cane. Otis was still favoring his right leg, which had been broken above the knee by a round from Josie Dobbs' deer rifle.

"Later, Mose."

"Mind how ya go."

Considering it later, Otis figured he could have handled the situation better. However, the larger boy, on his backswing, had raked the police chief of Hercules, Wisconsin, across the bridge of his nose. As often as he had been hit in the face over the years, Otis had never been able to subdue the childish sense of vulnerability triggered by a sucker punch. Instinct took over, and he became, for a moment, a cornered animal. He lashed out, seizing the whip hand, twisting it 'til the kid dropped the switch. Otis didn't relent his grip and stop shaking the boy 'til he heard him screaming.

"Lemme go, lemme go, lemme GO!"

Otis released him suddenly enough that the boy staggered and fell, landing hard on his butt. The boy's next utterance was somewhat of a surprise.

"Fuckin' cop. My mom's gonna sue you."

Otis had no reply.

"You keep your fuckin' hands off me, you prick. I'll kill you, ya son of a bitch. Kill ya!"

As Otis opened his mouth to reproach the young man for his language, the boy broke away, sprinting east on Main Street, pausing just long enough to raise a middle finger and shout, "Fuck you!"

Regaining his composure, Otis regarded the other boy, who was weeping silently. When Otis reached down to help him, the boy crept backward, bumped into the curb and clambered unaided to his feet. Otis noted the fiery welts on the boy's bare arms, already beginning to swell.

"That must hurt."

The boy's face was smeared with tears. Shame radiated from him like heat. He kept his eyes lowered. "Yeah, well ..."

Otis sensed in the boy the urge to flee. Before he could escape, Otis asked, "The kid who was hitting you, who was he?"

The answer was a low mumble, barely discernible. "Riley Hawkins."

As soon as Otis took a step toward the boy, he was on the move and down the block, his body still bent defensively. Otis remembered the feeling.

"Riley Hawkins," Otis said to himself. He suspected that he might hear the name again.

CHAPTER 2

As he ran, Riley Hawkins could feel his body shaking with emotion. The anger that had erupted in curses had turned into fear—that the police chief would chase him, fear of lights and sirens, fear that he would be thrown in jail and his mother dragged to the police station, bewildered and tearful. Riley hated that. His mother was such a pussy.

But wasn't he just as much of a pussy? Wasn't he running? Wasn't he afraid?

Too rushed to look back, Riley ducked onto Monroe Street, then turned—still going full-tilt and gasping for breath—down the unpaved alley behind Main. He ran 'til the alley ended at School Street. He slowed and tried to walk toward Main Street like nothing was wrong, looking cool even as his hands trembled, past the Kwik Trip and the bus depot. His eyes searched for a place where he could hide 'til the heat was off.

There!

He stopped before a two-story hulk, its brick chipped and blackened by time. Riley could still read the faded sign that stretched along the top of the first floor. "Quality," it said, followed by "S&Q HARDWARE," then "Service". The store had been closed, and all its windows broken, since before Riley could remember. Plywood sheets along the storefront had been there so long that their edges were frayed and curling. Several panels were tilted and threatening to tumble onto the sidewalk.

The defunct hardware store would be refuge, but there was no easy access. He could try to pull away one of the plywood panels, but people might notice the noise and dust. They might call up that asshole cop.

Riley studied the building. There were windows above. People used to live there. They went upstairs—there it was—through a door on the left side of the building.

The door was ajar.

Riley looked around. This end of town wasn't busy. He saw nobody coming along the street. A few people outside the bus depot paid no attention to Riley. He hurried across the sidewalk and slipped into the shallow entryway. He waited a moment on the threshold, reading his body, giving his nerves time to unjangle. Other kids viewed Riley as a sort of wolf, prowling and cruel. He never betrayed any sign of weakness. He had trained himself to conceal the waves of panic that would suddenly rise from his guts and flood his throat 'til he thought he would choke to death.

Riley waited. His panic simmered, then receded. He tried the door to the derelict building. It creaked as he pulled. He stopped when the opening was wide enough for him to squeeze through. He slid inside.

He faced a black void. There had to be a staircase, but he couldn't see it. Riley paused for his eyes to adjust.

There!

Somewhere above, the roof had split, allowing a sliver of sunlight. Faintly, Riley could see the stairs, grayish wood with rotten rubber treads peeling away. The acid smell of dust and wet rot filled his head. At his feet, the foyer, no more than four feet to the first step, was black, invisible.

The darkness before Riley was palpable. It told him to turn back and run. But the abandoned spaces upstairs stirred his urge to transgress, to break and enter, to find what's up there, what nobody else knows.

What a hideout this place could be.

Blindly, Riley went ahead and—holy shit!—down. There was no floor. Nothing beneath but an abyss. Riley plunged, wreathed in a clinging dampness. Bug-eyed and gasping for the breath that would allow a scream, the boy passed glints of light that, when he reached out at them, cut his fingers. He felt blood running on his skin. He was flying down a well of knives, a hand ripped open, a flailing leg torn into shreds. He cried out but only made a croaking sound, like a frog being strangled.

Headfirst, he dropped endlessly, miles and miles into black emptiness, slashed and ravaged by the stabbing walls, until ...

There!

He saw light, a twinkling array, like Christmas, arrayed in a circle that hurried toward his writhing descent. The closer he fell, the clearer he saw lights, some bright pinpoints and others dull blobs that shone from a surface that seemed to crawl. Closer still, and these were not incandescence but reflection of a glow from somewhere, an ominous shining that lit the tips of a stalagmite horror, razor spikes awaiting the boy, jutting up from a carpet of bodies impaled, some still alive, their white-rimmed eyes searching the darkness, blades piercing silent mouths.

As he waved his bleeding hands helplessly, desperate for purchase, gaping at a dark lagoon of squirming human meat, he saw one face clearly, skin yellowed, eyes sunk deep into its skull, a face he knew but had not seen for five years. Spikes spearing the apparition's neck, knives piercing his heart, his guts, his face, razor edges tearing at his flesh, Riley would be hitting bottom atop the body of his dead father.

As the spikes rushed toward him, Riley managed a last word.

"Noooooooooooo!"

His jaw banged on the floor, snapping his teeth together, and raising a puff of dust around his face. Riley looked around. The staircase, still vague and shadowy, was there, in front of him.

There was floor, filthy beneath, walls on either side. Riley clambered to his feet, shuddering, clutching at his clothes to feel for ripped fabric, peering at his bloodied hands.

There was no blood. He staggered backward, bumped the door, felt his way and stumbled into sunlight. Backing away, he stared at the door, cocking his head toward the dark slant he had just escaped.

"What the fuck," he whispered to himself.

He hurried away, straight down Main, unconcerned with the cop's whereabouts, aware of no one. He brushed dust off his clothes and ran his hands over his body once more, just to be sure. He turned and studied the old S&Q building, which looked the same—rundown and doomed.

Riley Hawkins realized something about that place that nobody else knew. He could use it. This might be fun.

CHAPTER 3

(Friday, the 23rd of May)

Carol Demeter set down her coffee cup with a thunk forceful enough that a few drops hopped onto the formica tabletop. She was across from Jim Otis in a window booth at Calamity Jane's, the only diner in Hercules.

"What?" asked Otis.

Carol fixed him with the sort of stare that snakes use on field mice. "June, you know," she said, "is imminent."

"Imminent?" asked Otis.

Carol was an English teacher.

"Yes," she replied. "It's right around the damn corner, Fosdick."

Otis sensed her direction but hesitated to follow. "Ah, the lazy, hazy, crazy days of summer," he said. "Who recorded that? Sam Cooke?"

"Nat Cole," said Maisie Hopkins, a world-class eavesdropper who had arrived with a coffee pot. She poured.

"Oh, right," said Otis.

"Carol's talking about weddings." Maisie had no compunctions about giving unsolicited advice. "People get married in June."

Carol, remaining silent, intensified her serpentine stare.

"But you see the problem," Otis said, turning to Maisie. "June's too soon. All the arrangements take weeks, months. I know this. I've been married before."

"It ain't too soon, Jimmy, if you just do it in the courthouse over in La Crosse," Maisie replied. "Blood test today. Hitched on Monday."

Otis lowered his head. "Jesus," he muttered.

Carol relented, laying a hand on Otis' arm. "That would be fine with me, Maisie. But my mother would disown me. She wants the full catastrophe—church, vows, flowers, white gown, big cake, polka band."

Maisie nodded. "So, July?"

Otis cringed. Carol laughed. Maisie left.

Otis and Carol worked quietly on breakfast long enough for the subject to change.

"Word is," said Carol, "you were chasing a little kid down Main Street yesterday."

"I didn't chase him. Didn't try. He was fast and I'm crippled."

"All right, he got away. But what did he do to deserve being chased?"

"He was beating on another kid with, um ... a willow switch."

"Really? Those things hurt like crazy. My big brother used to—"

"I asked a few people," Otis broke in. "The kid's name, the one whipping the other kid, is Riley Hawkins."

Carol lifted an eyebrow. "Aha."

"You know who he is?"

Carol said, "Every teacher in the system knows about Riley. They dread the day he walks into their class."

"Is he that bad?"

"Bad? That's too simple," said Carol. "There are stories that circulate. He explodes. Beats up another boy. Throws a book at his teacher. Breaks windows. He gets suspended. He comes back to school, doesn't make trouble for months. Then, kaboom."

"Why don't they just expel him?"

Carol sighed. "Where would he go? Private school? We don't have one in Hercules. And Riley's mother couldn't pay for it. She waits tables at the brewhouse over in Hillsboro."

"No father?"

"Disappeared when the kid was five or six."

Otis nodded.

"Riley told one of his teachers, Helene Rinaldi—you've met her. Remember?"

"Sort of. Red hair, right?"

"Brown."

"Oh, right."

"Anyway," Carol pressed on, "Riley told Helene that his father was dead. Murdered."

"Murdered?"

"Yes, in Beloit."

"Why Beloit?"

"No idea," said Carol. "But Riley's story was pretty elaborate. He said his father was attacked by black gangsters with knives. They tore him apart and threw him in the Rock River, never to be seen again."

"That's Riley's story?"

"That's what he told Helene."

"But?"

"There was no murder. Jerry Hawkins was a bum, drunk, violent, beat his wife and finally just took off. Thank God."

Otis shook his head. "Welcome to Mayberry," he said forlornly.

Maisie was back, with more coffee. Somehow, she had overheard Riley Hawkins' name. She said, "Duane, my dearly beloved, he had Riley in Little League. He could pitch. Had a great arm."

"But?" asked Otis.

"Well, he kept throwing his fastball at other kids' heads," said Maisie as she refilled cups. "Duane had to kick him out of the league."

Otis' phone started to vibrate on the tabletop. He looked at the screen. It read, "Natalie."

He answered. "Hiya, kid." He put the phone on speaker.

"So, Daddy, it's almost June!"

Otis knew what was coming.

"People get married in June," said Natalie.

Carol laughed.

"Shit," mumbled Otis.

"Daddy, you shouldn't say 'shit' in front of your daughter."

Otis didn't reply.

"Carol," said Natalie, "are you there?"

"Yes."

"Me, too," said Maisie.

"Carol, I've got dibs on maid of honor."

"That goes without saying, Nat," said Carol. "But don't count on a June wedding."

"Daddy's got cold feet?"

"Icy," said Maisie.

Otis was the only member of the conversation not laughing.

"So, July?" asked Natalie.

Otis broke in, "Shouldn't you be on your way to school?"

"On my way, Daddy. Love you. You, too, Carol."

The call disconnected.

On her way back to the kitchen, Maisie said, "You don't deserve that girl, Chief."

"Nobody does," he said to himself. "I'm thinking about a nunnery."

CHAPTER 4

Riley Hawkins had pitched a story hard to resist. Shane Klosterman, flattered by the attention of a classmate who usually tormented him, believed Riley eagerly. Upstairs at the old S&Q Hardware building, there was an old lady who died. She had stuffed her mattress full of money. The mattress was still there, full of treasure, thousands of dollars.

Shane might have asked Riley why no one had gone into the old lady's apartment to clear it out, and why they didn't find the money. He might have logically wondered why Riley was sharing this secret when he could have gone upstairs and claimed the loot for himself. But Shane, eleven years old, was disinclined to skepticism.

He followed Riley to the decrepit S&Q building after school. He paused before the tilted door and its narrow opening.

"Ya scared?" taunted Riley.

"Aw, no," said Shane. "But it's dark. I can't see anything."

"Ya gotta go inside first. There's light up above."

Riley gave Shane a shove.

Once inside, Shane teetered a few seconds on the edge of the entryway, staring into blackness. He took a step, expecting to feel floorboards beneath his foot. But it was sand, sand that flew up in a hissing rush, blinding him. For what might have been a minute or an hour, he peered sightless into an oblivion darker than the lightless staircase. He would scream but the sand entered his mouth and sifted into his throat. When he could see again, through a gray luminescence, he couldn't move. It took him a long, bewildering moment to realize that somehow he had been buried up to his neck, in a pit of crawling, squirmy sand. He could feel no bottom. He couldn't feel his feet.

The sand was blowing, stinging his face, piling up below his mouth, coating his teeth, creeping toward his nose. He coughed it up and spit it out, but it came back, alive and relentless.

Shane uttered a frantic whine as he tried to move hands that were pinned by the pressure of the wormy earth. The sand pressed into his chest like a giant hand, forcing him to breathe shallowly, to sense the onset of suffocation. As long as he could remember, Shane had awakened from nightmares of being sealed in boxes, gasping for his last breath as he clawed at lacquered walls. Night upon night, he had sat up suddenly in bed waving torn fingers at dirt that had been piled upon him, six feet underground, dirt pressing his eyes shut, drowning his cries as it poured into his mouth and filled his lungs.

He tried to turn his head, to look for help, for someone. There was only sand, stretching for miles, gray, empty and lifeless but moving, closing in on him. If he called, maybe someone too far away to see would come to help. But he was terrified and he had lost his voice. Sucking for air, squeezing his eyes shut, he fought the panic that crackled in his head and clutched his guts. He opened his eyes. There might be someone. Where was Riley?

Shane opened his mouth to cry for help. He hadn't noticed the insects before. Where did they come from, praying mantises, each one as big as his hand, green, brown, black, with claws that waved and clacked? They had been waiting at his lips. They rushed inside, scrabbling onto his tongue, gnawing ravenously at the tender flesh inside his cheeks. Shane gurgled in terror. He strained against the straitjacket of sand, feeling his muscles rip. Tears ran down his face, snot poured from his nose. He could feel the mantises as they scurried, jockeying against each other, toward his throat, hungry to start chewing his lungs and eating his heart, killing him inside before the crushing sand could kill him on the outside. He clamped his mouth shut to crush the little monsters. In death, the mantises loosed a burst of boiling blood that sent a searing, melting pain that went to his brain like a shower of needles.

Shane coughed. He gagged up the crushed bodies and chewed the legs of the bugs. He drank all the slime that was blocking his voice and then, raging against the death he had imagined all his life in the worst of his dreams, he uttered a scream that rebounded in dust and retching.

Shane lay on the dirty floor just inside the door. His mouth was full of bitter-tasting grit. He saw the light outside and crawled desperately.

"So," said Riley, who was leaning against the wall, eating M&Ms, "wha'd ya see?"

CHAPTER 5

Friday night at A'Jay's was always hopping. The farmers came into town, and the GIs stationed at Fort McCoy started their weekend furloughs by filling every bar within a fifty-mile radius. A'Jay's drew a disproportionate share of African-American non-coms because the owner, A.J. Cartwright, was black.

So, the place was full. And loud.

Regardless of the crowd, the end of the bar was off-limits to transients. A.J. saved that corner for Police Chief Jim Otis and a coterie of regulars, including Otis' squeeze, Carol Demeter. Typically outspoken among the company was Crystal MacDougal, a vicarious relic of the Sixties who had just missed the Sixties but who embodied its spirit more authentically than the shriveled husk that remained of Wavy Gravy. Crystal had chosen to wear, from her extensive wardrobe, a baggy-sleeved coat of many colors over a nylon lavender T. Her three-quarter-length purple toreador pants reached to the top of a pair of hand-tooled acanthus-pattern white Tecovas boots. Her drink was Johnnie Walker Blue, the most expensive bottle in the house.

Hap Schaller, the town's only master plumber, was drinking his usual Pabst Blue Ribbon. He had stood Kenny Kelly a round of vodka and was now regretting his generosity because

Kenny had finished his drink in less than a second and was lobbying for more. Kenny kept an account at A'Jay's but tended to exhaust his balance toward the end of the month and so, in his only sign of prudence, cadged from anyone who got within panhandling range.

Usually, Maury Higginson, one of Hercules' two auxiliary cops, dropped in for a pint of Spotted Cow after finishing a patrol shift. He was on the other side of Kenny, serving—not very willingly—to help keep Kenny upright.

Minnie Trout, Jim Otis' indispensable dispatcher, was closest to Carol, sipping a Sambuca that A.J. had warmed in the microwave and garnished with a coffee bean. Minnie wasn't as regular as some of the other habitués, but she showed when she anticipated a topic that would add to her mental encyclopedia of local lore.

Mose Irons, another occasional visitor, was only present because he felt like a whiskey sour. Nevertheless, he was the member of the company with the most relevant commentary on the evening's topic. "I knew a fella, Clancy, happily married, worked in a bank, had kids and the usual dog," said Mose. "Spent a weekend every month or so training with the Army Reserve. Never expected active duty. Then Desert Storm comes along and he gets called up. Five months in the desert sweating bullets, dispatching trucks and desperate for a clean toilet. Meanwhile, his wife gets lonely and decides to have an adventure. Her adventure turns out to be a farm implements tycoon named Elgar who sweeps Phyllis off her feet, swathes her in silk and takes her on a three-weeks tour of London, Paris and Istanbul. Clancy has no idea, comes home to an empty house. Phyllis and the kids are three towns up the road, living in a McMansion with Elgar. Clancy's neighbor comes over. He's been takin' care of the dog. He tells Clancy about the lightning romance of Elgar and Phyllis, which is all news to Clancy, because he hadn't heard a word from her in three months.

"Another three months go by, and the poor sap is divorced. Three months later, he takes his little boy to the county fair, where there's one of those games where you throw plastic rings at a lot of Coke bottles. And while the boy's tossin' rings, his dad's warming up to this carny gal in the booth, who's quite fetching, a real cutie. The guy ends up spendin' twenty bucks there, the girl gives the boy a big stuffed bunny and, later that night, the poor divorced putz is meeting the cutie at the closest motel to the fairgrounds. Two weeks later, he's married to her, and six months after that, he's payin' the little gold-digger half his salary in alimony. By this time, the carny girl has followed in Phyllis' high-heel, hightailin' footsteps. She's shackin' up with her brother's marijuana supplier. Course, after all this, poor ol' Clancy's tapped out and living in a sixteen-foot Airstream camper."

"Jesus," said Maury.

"What about the dog?" asked Kenny.

"What's your point, Mose?" said Crystal.

"What I'm gettin' at, hon, is the mortal peril of the rebound marriage."

"Rebound?" growled Carol. "We're talking about basketball?"

"We're talking about guilt," said Mose, pausing to sip his sour. "Nine times out of ten, when a man's marriage fails, he starts lookin' back for what went wrong and he tends to decide it was his fault."

"Mose, I looked back," said Otis. "It *was* my fault."

Mose cocked his head and allowed an ironic smirk. "I'll take that under advisement, Jim."

"What Mose is saying," offered Crystal, "is that this divorced putz was trying to purge his sins by getting married again as fast as he could. On the rebound."

Mose nodded.

"Wait a minute," said Minnie, nodding toward Otis. "Carol, how long have you known this divorced putz?"

Carol smiled, "Two and a half years."

"Divorced putz?" asked Otis.

"So, how long is it gonna take for this rebound to come down?" asked Minnie.

Crystal hit Otis with a motherly glare. "She's asking, Jimmy, why can't you get off the pot and set a date?"

"Is that a mixed metaphor?" said Otis to Carol.

"Answer the question," Carol replied.

"Ouch," said Maury.

Otis exhaled lengthily.

"Okay," he said. "For some reason this woman—this excellent, exceptionally attractive and intelligent woman ..."

Otis paused to let everyone drink in Carol's loveliness. She shrank slightly in the spotlight.

"... has consented to marry me. I can't figure out why. Has Mose mentioned that I'm developing a bald spot?"

"Wait," said Crystal. "You're saying that Carol—not you—should have second thoughts about this marriage because you're not worthy of her?"

"Talk about horseshit," said Maury.

"I'm just wondering," said Otis, "if she really knows what she's getting—"

Otis' mobile phone started to buzz on the bar. He looked at the display.

"It's Nat."

"Saved by the bell," said Crystal.

Otis put his phone on speaker. "Hiya, kid," he said.

"Daddy, are you at A'Jay's?"

She was greeted by a chorus of hellos.

"Where are you?" asked Otis.

"Oh, I'm at home. Debbie's staying over."

Another voice came faintly from the phone, "Hi, everyone," said Debbie Albright, Natalie's BFF.

"So, what's happening?" asked Natalie.

"The usual Friday night riot," said A.J., breaking for a moment from his duties." How're you, babe?"

"I'm good, A.J.," said Natalie. "But I'm worried."

"About what?" asked Crystal.

"Well, you know." Natalie's voice, even in the dull roar of the tavern, was noticeably coy. "How my poor dad is all alone in the world. No one to take care of him."

"Oh, for Christ's sake," said Otis. "I'm hangin' up."

He didn't hang up.

"Not saved by the bell, after all," said Minnie.

"Look, kid," said Otis, "I get enough grief from this crowd. I don't need you piling on."

"Daddy, I'm just saying, you gotta decide."

"Yeah," said Debbie, in the background.

"Yeah," said Kenny. "Piss or get off."

"For once, I agree with Kenny," said Carol.

"Daddy," said Natalie, in her most therapeutic tone, "you love Carol, right?"

Otis sighed and scanned the company, stopping at Carol, whose brow wrinkled in anticipation.

"Daddy?"

"Well, yes. Yeah, of course I do."

"You could've answered faster, Fosdick," said Carol.

"Fuckin' A," muttered Kenny.

"Carol," said Natalie, "you love my dad?"

"Yes, I do," said Carol. "God help me."

"Well then, jeez, Daddy, come on! I wanna be a maid of honor! What's your problem?"

"He's scared," said Maury, muscling in.

"My daddy scared?" Natalie was incredulous. "Of what?"

"Being hit by the rebound," said Maury.

Natalie was silent for a moment. "Carol," she said finally, "what's he talking about?"

"Well, Nat," Carol said. "Mose was saying—"

"Is Mose there?" asked Natalie, excitedly.

"Yeah, here I am, sweetheart."

The conversation paused while Natalie had a moment of mutual admiration with the town's avuncular barber and resident philosopher.

"May I go on?" asked Carol at last.

"Oh, yeah, about rebounds," said Natalie. "Yes, yes, please."

"Well, Nat, Mose was telling us about a man who felt so guilty about failing in his marriage that he rushed to remarry as fast as he could."

"On the rebound," said Maury helpfully.

"Oh, I know," said Natalie. "And he married the wrong woman!"

"Yes."

"And he made himself even more miserable."

"Yes."

"But you're *not* the wrong woman."

"Thank you, Natalie."

"Daddy, don't you know that?"

"I know it, kid."

"Carol's the *right* woman."

"Yes, she is."

"Well then, dammit, Daddy ... Wait!"

The phone sank into a pregnant silence. Seven people, minus A.J.—who was mixing drinks—stared at the screen.

"I get it," said Natalie.

"You do?" asked Otis.

"Oh, Daddy, I remember how it was when you and Mom were breaking up. Whenever you came over, it was like a funeral home. Mom was so angry. She just sat there waiting for you to say something—anything—so she could just jump down your throat and tell you that you were such a son of a bitch. And you just stood there and let her do it. Daddy, you turned into a *mouse*."

"Ouch," said Maury.

"Because he felt guilty," said Crystal.

"Goddammit, I was guilty," said Otis.

"Oh, Daddy, c'mon. You didn't kill anybody," Natalie said. "You gotta get over it."

"Wiser words were never spoken," intoned Mose softly.

"Nat."

"Quiet, Daddy," said Natalie. "You know what you need?"

Otis was trapped. All eyes focused on him, including Carol's. He was being scolded by a fourteen-year-old.

"Okay, kid. I give up. Tell me what I need."

"Daddy, you need a house without guilt."

This gave Otis pause. "A house—"

"Daddy, think about it. Even before Mom knew what was going on with you and ... you know, your secret lover, well, *you knew*. Right?"

"Secret lover?"

"And you felt bad. Right?"

"Uh huh."

"For a long time. Right?"

Otis grunted affirmatively.

"So, every time you came home, you felt guilty. You were cheating on Mom. You lived in a house of guilt."

"Well," said Minnie, "that's good."

"Smart girl," said A.J., who had returned.

Otis felt himself shrinking. "Nat, what's your point?"

"Daddy, you should live together. You and Carol. It's the twenty-first century."

"Wait a minute," said Carol.

Natalie did not wait a minute.

"Daddy, you need to come home to a house where you don't feel guilty. You need to come home to love. You need Carol in your house, all the time."

"Well now," said Crystal.

Carol was gulping her wine.

"The young lady is talking about catharsis," said Mose.

"The prodigal husband is welcomed back into a loving fold. The sins and recriminations are cleansed from his soul and purged from his memory."

"Wait. You want me to move in with this man?"

"Well," said Maury, "you were gonna marry 'im, weren'tcha?"

"Yes, but this is different!" said Carol.

"No, Carol!" Natalie insisted. "It's orientation. Like your first day in high school. You're scared at first, but you get used to it in a little while."

Crystal patted Otis on the hand. "I love that kid."

Natalie heard. "I love you, too, Crys."

Otis had regained an inch or two in height. "Y'know," he said close to Carol's ear, "it's not a bad idea."

Natalie heard. "I toldja, Daddy!"

"Quiet now," said Otis.

"I have to think about this," said Carol.

"Think of the rent you'll save," said A.J.

"This is not about money, ya big lug," snapped Minnie.

"Ev'rything's about money," croaked Kenny.

Otis held up a hand. "Okay, let's stop right here, please," he said. "This is a big decision."

"But you were already gonna marry her, f'Chrissake," said Maury.

"Yes, but marriage," said Mose, "that's somewhere off in the future. It offers the security of hypothesis. Moving in together? You can do that this weekend."

"No, no! You can't," came the voice of Natalie. "Not this weekend. I wanna be there. I wanna help."

Carol had slipped into a reflective silence, cradling her glass and staring into the wine. The others sensed her mood and quieted. Otis took the phone off speaker, spoke softly to his daughter and said goodbye.

The group groped for a change of subject.

Since his termination from the Chicago police and the end of his marriage to Connie, followed by several alcoholic months of self-pity, Jim Otis had been mostly scrupulous about a two-beer limit. As A.J. delivered Otis' second black and tan, he said, "I heard you were out on Main Street the other day whipping Riley Hawkins with a willow switch."

"What?"

"That's the word around town."

"No. Wait. I wasn't—"

"Hey, don't feel bad. The town's on your side for a change. Everybody figures the little shit deserves a good whipping."

"But I didn't."

"Probably not."

Mose intervened, testifying to Otis' innocence. This gave Otis occasion to ask A.J. about Riley Hawkins. A.J. deferred to Minnie.

"He's a hellion," she said.

"I like that word," said Carol.

"The boy was in first grade when his father ... Crys, what was his name?"

"Jerry."

"That's right. Jerry got tired of beating the hell out of Beth, Riley's mother, and took a powder. This was lucky for the boy, because his dad was probably knocking him around already. It was bound to get worse."

"So, the boy was schooled in violence," said Carol.

"Oh, but smart. Cunning," said Minnie. "The other kids, even older ones, they keep a weather eye out for him."

"I know a few teachers who've had him in class," said Carol. "One said he's like a reptile, with thick skin that changes colors and blends into the background. You never know if he's going to bite a chunk out of you or lick your face like a puppy. Beneath the camouflage, you don't know what's inside."

"Well, the Riley Hawkins I met wasn't much of a puppy," said Otis.

"As he gets older," said Minnie, "my guess is that the puppy turns pit bull."

On their way to Otis' car, Carol was distant.

"What Natalie said," Otis ventured. "About us ... you know ..."

"We need to sleep on it."

"Together?"

Carol reached for Otis' hand.

CHAPTER 6

(Monday, the 26th of May)

Uncharacteristically, Riley Hawkins approached Amy Caruthers with an air of deference. Most boys didn't approach the prettiest girl in the sixth grade at all. Her beauty, even at age eleven, was scary. Her wits were even scarier. But Amy was just the sort of classmate to whom he wanted to shove off the stairs at the old building.

In the hallway, just outside Ms. Wick's classroom, Riley tapped Amy on the arm.

She spun and pierced Riley with her eyes.

"What do *you* want?" she said, with a note of accusation that Riley knew all too well.

"I was jist wond'rin'," said Riley, "if you wanna see somethin'."

"I see things all the time, Riley. I've got eyes." She began to turn, heading into class.

"Not like this," said Riley.

She paused.

"Not like anything you ever saw."

Amy squinched her eyes. "Oh yeah? What?"

Riley had her.

"I can't tell ya. I gotta show ya."

Amy had a final defense against her growing curiosity. "Why me?"

"Shit, you're smarter'n everybody," said Riley. "You might be able to figure it out."

"Figure *what* out?"

"I gotta *show* ya."

The bell rang, and Amy dashed to her desk.

By the end of the school day, Amy had succumbed to her curiosity. She agreed, although maintaining an air of dignified reluctance, to meet Riley at the Kwik Trip. A half-hour later, he saw her coming, in a blue dress cinched around the waist with a flower-print scarf. She looked so nice. He had second thoughts about sending her toward the dark staircase.

She strode up to Riley and stopped too close, rising on tiptoes to stare the boy in the eye. "This better be good," she said coldly.

Riley's resolve returned. He guided her toward the derelict building. As they approached the doorway, Amy said, "It's in there?"

"Yeah."

Amy paused at the curb, scanning the building, reading the faded S&Q sign. She said, "They call it the Kuckuck building."

"The what?"

"The Kuckuck building."

"Who?"

"Grownups."

"Kuckuck?"

"Yes."

"What's that mean?"

"Don't know."

Amy moved toward the door. "We go through there?"

Riley held back. "You first," he said casually.

He had a feeling about Amy Caruthers. She had what Riley's grandmother called moxie. She wouldn't hesitate to be first into a dark tunnel.

"Okay," said Amy.

She had to lower her head and twist to fit through the tilted door. An almost choking smell of oil and dust froze her for a moment. But she couldn't back off. Riley—the class bully and a total creep—was watching.

When Amy's foot reached out for the black floor beneath, it kept reaching, 'til Amy couldn't balance. She fell forward, in a sudden, disorienting, helpless somersault. She opened her mouth to cry out to Riley, but it filled with water—no, oil. No! Oil, and water, too, and tendrils of slime she could feel curling on her skin. She was plunging headfirst into a liquid abyss.

As she flapped her arms desperately, holding her breath, struggling to turn herself upright, to reverse this dive into oblivion, Amy remembered the worst day in her life, at a pool in La Crosse. Her first—last!—swimming lesson. The pool was outdoors, the water like ice. "Put your face in the water," the teacher shouted. No! She couldn't. She was paralyzed. She would drown. She would die, choking. Can't breathe. Her eyes going black. Her chest an implosion of pain. The teacher came. "Put your face in the water." No! I can't! A hand on her head, pushing. The hand was huge and strong. She could fight, splash, twist and struggle, but she was helpless. Her face in the water, trapped, lungs sucking in the whole pool, water pushed out in a panicked, ululating cry. She floundered, she clawed at the killing hand, screaming, gasping, choking, screaming 'til the hand relented. And she blundered, sobbing and gagging, out of the pool, running then, running 'til she was outside, on the sidewalk, still in her swimsuit, where she vomited pool water and bile and then sat, in a puddle, crying uncontrollably for her mother. Her mother came and took her home, never brought her back.

Amy couldn't swim. Her lungs were wracked with the pain of holding her breath. She flopped and swirled, looking up finally—at nothing. It was black above, black below. She reached up. A finger felt air. There was a surface. She swept her arms downward instinctively. She kicked. There was air above. No! A hand, she couldn't see it. She felt it, seizing her head, tangling oily fingers in her hair, pushing. Pushing Amy. Pushing down! No!

She opened her mouth to scream, to drown, to die screaming. Tendrils of slime poured into her, soiling her tongue with a flavor like the smell of shit. They flowed into her throat, reaching for her windpipe, plunging into her lungs, hungry to fill, thirsty to kill. With her last sliver of strength, she stretched a finger upward, somewhere. It touched. An edge!

Amy hit the floor with both knees. A stab of pain shot up one leg. She lurched to her feet. Her palms were scraped and coated with stinging dust. In the thin light from the outside, she saw blood running down her leg.

Amy came out of the broken doorway after barely a minute inside. Like the others, like Riley himself had been, she was dirty and stunned, her hair flying in all directions. She was bleeding from her knee, from something sharp on the floor. Her eyes were glazed. He went up to her and asked the same question he had asked Shane Klosterman.

"Wha'd ya see, Amy?"

He expected nothing from her. Shane had run away, silently. The whitened blankness of the other boy's face told Riley that Shane would never talk about what had happened in there. Shane hadn't been in school on Monday.

For a while, Amy was still. She breathed hungrily, drinking the air, not speaking, not likely to speak. Riley asked again, "Wha'd ya see?"

Amy reached out and held Riley by the front of his shirt. Focus came back to her eyes. Hurt and malice radiated from them. She spoke.

"How did you do that?"

"Do what?" said Riley. "I didn' do nothin'. It's that place."

"That place," repeated Amy, loosing her grip on Riley.

"There's somethin' there," said Riley.

"What?"

"Jeez, I don' know, Amy. Whatever it is, it don't want anybody in there. It don't want ya t'go upstairs."

They both turned and looked at the crooked door into the blackness beyond.

"Why?" Amy asked.

"I don' know."

Riley tried again.

"Wha'd ya see?"

"See?" said Amy. She took time to regain her mind. "What I was afraid of."

She waited for more words to form. They came slowly. Finally, she said, "What I was most afraid of, in the whole world."

Amy turned back to Riley. "Don't you do that again," she said. "Don't do that to anybody else."

Riley lied. "Uh huh," he said.

CHAPTER 7

(Tuesday, the 27th of May)

Jim Otis had dispatched his deputy, Earl Schober, to monitor the goings-on at the city council meeting. Earl, sitting as unobtrusively as he could manage—in the sparsely populated spectator section of the large City Hall meeting room—was beginning to doze off. Council Chairman Roland J. "Digger" Cedarfield turned a page of the evening's agenda and said, "Okay, gang, we're up to Old Business."

He peered at the page. "Hm, let's see ... ah! Is the police chief here?"

Everyone knew that Otis was not present, but Cedarfield made a show of peering around the overlit room. He fixed on Earl and spoke sharply.

Earl, vaguely aware that his name had been uttered, opened his eyes a slit and looked around.

"Earl!" Cedarfield repeated, more audibly.

Earl lurched in his seat and sat up straight.

"Oh," said Earl. "Sorry. I had to work a double shift yesterday. Didn't get much sleep. Teddy Gilbert had t'go up to Madison, for his LESB—"

Cedarfield broke in, "Earl, we're getting complaints about the Kuckuck building."

"Oh," said Earl, "that old hardware store. Wasn't the town s'posed to tear that down?"

The eyes of the council turned reflexively toward Mayor Luke Winstead, whose table was situated at a right angle to the council.

"The Kuckuck demolition was in the budget, Digger," he said, with a faint air of apology. "But we had to shift some money into snow removal."

"Oh yeah," said Earl. "Hell of a winter."

"Earl," said Cedarfield, regaining command, "we've been getting calls. According to Lester Munk at the bus depot—"

"Lester called me twice," said Councilwoman Gloria Osterholm."

"About the Kuckuck building," Cedarfield amended.

"He did, really?" said Earl. "How come?"

"Lester said he saw kids going in there," said Gloria.

"That's a dangerous building," said Councilman Abe Jaffe. "It's been condemned for ten years. We should've torn it down a long time ago."

"Well, we appropriated the money," said the mayor.

"But it snowed," said Earl helpfully.

Cedarfield scowled at Earl, as though both winter weather and the trespass at the Kuckuck building were his fault.

Luke Winstead injected a note of alarm. "We can't let anyone get in there, kids or anybody. It's a matter of liability," he said. "Technically, the town owns the building. If somebody gets hurt ..."

"You mean," said Earl serenely, "you want the Police Department to keep kids out of that building."

"That's right, Earl," said Cedarfield.

"It's a matter of liability," Winstead reiterated.

"So, it's the police's job 'til the town gets around to tearin' it down," added Earl. "Right?"

No one on the council replied.

Earl nodded affirmatively and winked at the chairman. "We'll watch it like a hawk, Digger."

Cedarfield grunted dubiously.

It was past eleven when Earl Schober pushed through the door at A'Jay's and settled onto a stool next to Hap Schaller, who was soiled, wet and aromatic.

"Jesus, Hap, what happened t'you?"

"Sewer connection ruptured up on Achilles. You know the Grindls, Bruce and Kirsten?"

"Course I do."

"Well, I was out there tonight, diggin' up their yard, lookin' for the goddamn busted pipe. I'd've gone home, but Dinah ain't gonna let me in the house in this condition. She's gonna make me undress out on the lawn, all the way down t'my Jockey shorts. And then she's gonna hose me down," said Hap.

Kenny, two stools over, staring at an empty glass and trying to make eye contact with A.J., muttered, "Jesus, last time I got hosed down by a woman. Must've been ..."

He didn't finish.

"Anyway," Hap concluded, "I needed a drink first."

He was sipping a double shot of Dewar's with a PBR back.

A.J., without asking, delivered Earl his pint of Leinenkugel Red and provided Kenny with a vodka double.

Without being asked about it, Earl informed A.J. and Hap that he had had city council duty.

"Well, sir," said A.J., "you have my sympathy."

"Ain't that Jim's job?" asked Hap.

"He had a date," said Earl.

A.J. added to the report. "Carol wanted to check out that fancy new restaurant in Madison. The Harvey House."

"Oh, an intimate dinner."

A.J. smiled. "Yeah, with Carol's mother as chaperone."

Earl killed a quarter of his pint and looked at A.J. "So, what's the story about that fallin'-down building up by the bus depot. Used t'be a hardware store."

"The Kuckuck building," said A.J., slipping into his role as unofficial town historian. "It was probably already closed down and boarded up when you moved to Hercules, Earl."

Earl nodded.

"Well, Andy Sturtevant owned the S&Q Hardware. Ran it for twenty years or so. But as soon as he qualified for Social Security, he closed up shop and moved to Fort Myers."

"So, why's it called that. What's a Kuckuck?" Earl asked.

"The landlords, for about thirty years, were the Kuckuck sisters. Maye and Faye. Old maids. Lived like hermits over on Kilbourn in the old family house. They barely ever went out. They didn't have a car. Had all their groceries delivered from Burnstad's. They died within a month of each other and left no kin that anybody knew of. Not even a third cousin. The county had a hell of a time figuring out who exactly had claim to the Kuckuck building after the sisters passed. Sturtevant was still running the S&Q down below, and there were tenants up above. With nobody to collect their rent, Andy and the upstairs folks stayed on rent-free for more than a year. When the county finally deeded the building to the town, the council tried to collect back rent from the tenants who'd been living in the two drafty apartments upstairs. But they just folded up and moved out. Andy didn't pay anything either. He fought the town in court long enough to sell his house in Hercules and then he was off to Florida."

"Which leaves the town," observed Hap, "stuck with a condemned building and the bill for tearin' it down."

"And now," said Earl, "we got kids trampling in there, where one of 'em's gonna break a leg and the town'll have to pay the hospital bill."

"I assume," said A.J., "that Digger's on your case about that."

Earl nodded. "Yeah, well, Digger can go piss up a rope," he said. "Can I have another beer?"

CHAPTER 8

(Wednesday, the 28th of May)

As they left Calamity's, Otis opened the door for Carol. Breakfast had been quiet and thoughtful. They were reluctant to take seriously Natalie's advice on cohabitation, mostly because Nat was only fourteen. Nevertheless, the seed had been planted. They were leaning toward a trial roommate period in Otis' cabin. Their hesitancy was not a matter of logistics. Carol was already spending more than half her nights away from her duplex on Zeus Avenue. Her refrigerator wasn't stocked sufficiently to nourish a gerbil.

The barrier was psychological. They each needed time to surmount their misgivings after their own fashion. Meanwhile, they avoided the topic.

Carol stopped Otis at his car.

"Um," she said.

"Yes?"

"Speaking of Riley Hawkins."

"I wasn't."

"I know," said Carol. "But someone mentioned him in the faculty lounge."

"The *high school* faculty lounge?"

"Yes."

"But Riley's not in high school."

"That's true, Fosdick, but the kid's a popular topic. None of us are looking forward to him."

"Ah," said Otis. "So, what about Riley Hawkins?"

"Well, word is that he's scaring other kids."

"Scaring them? Like what, jumping out from behind trees and yelling 'Boo!'"

"I don't know. But whatever he's doing, it's bigger than 'boo'."

"I'm getting the impression," said Otis, "that this kid's gonna be my next law enforcement problem."

"Not if you set him straight."

Otis smiled ruefully. "You mean, take time off from trying to set myself straight?"

Carol smiled back. "Don't underestimate yourself, Fosdick. Riley's been without a father half his life. With kids like him, a big slob like you comes along and pays him a little attention, they start looking up to you. You fill a big hole in his life."

Otis' only answer was a dubious scowl.

"Besides," Carol added as she turned, "he reminds you of you."

She was inside her car and starting the engine before Otis could think of a retort.

"Oh yeah?" he muttered.

Otis wouldn't admit it, but Riley Hawkins had been on his mind ever since the boy's valedictory "Fuck you."

Not long after taking the job as police chief, Otis had come to realize that kids in a little town like Hercules get cubbyholed early in life. While a kid isn't looking, someone makes a life-defining decision. It might be a neighbor, a teacher or a gossip who absorbs every whisper and lie and turns it into local gospel. Most likely, this presumptive identity is conjured by another kid with a knack for spreading the word that a particular boy or girl possesses certain immutable qualities that fix the entire community's perceptions like a brand burned into skin. Once pegged as a brain or a beauty, as a fair-haired hero or as the hero's punching bag, the targeted kid has no escape. He—or she—is, for all time in the town of his birth and upbringing, what people say about him—or her. Otis noticed that kids thus labeled not only accept whatever status had been ordained to them, but they tend to live up to their reputation. They might have talents and aptitudes that they cannot perceive because they've come to see themselves, prematurely, through the frozen gaze of familiar strangers. Trapped in a role ordained by the community, these kids don't beat against their imaginary walls. Like bugs in a jar, they resign themselves to their confinement. Too many of them give up becoming different from what other kids say, different from what the whole town says, because they don't know how to grow outward. They don't know how to change.

As the town's police chief, Otis had more contact than most of Hercules' denizens with kids who'd been tagged as losers, stoners, dweebs and dead-enders. All of them passed through the Grove, or got bogged down in the Grove too long to save themselves. Most of them lived up to the town's lazy prejudice and simply, agreeably failed. Some lucky kids, like Tommy Meineke, one of Otis' onetime headaches, had escaped the town, wised up and changed their fate.

Almost at first glance, Otis sensed that Riley had no idea who he really was. Grownups who had dealt with him from early in his life had seen his hair-trigger temper and animal ferocity and decided he was trouble. He would come, they decided, to no good end. Otis saw the same qualities. Riley's hostility toward figures of authority told Otis that almost every grownup in the boy's life had tried to control him, rather than help, care for or listen to him. Otis also saw in Riley a feral cunning that suggested more intelligence than Riley's elders had yet to appreciate. Riley was driven by a fierce, almost reckless curiosity.

After more than a decade of largely futile contact with troubled kids, in the streets of Chicago and in the village of Hercules, Otis had no interest in reforming Riley Hawkins. The town had pegged Riley as a bully and a punk, and this brand had been seared into his psyche. He was probably already too old to fix. All Otis could do—which he always did with kids like Riley—was to show him the respect that few people had ever granted the boy.

CHAPTER 9

(Friday, the 30th of May)

Earl Schober had turned the graveyard-shift patrol over to Maury Higginson, and he felt entitled to a beer at A'Jay's before going home to Elaine. To get next to Otis at the end of the bar, Earl had to displace Kenny Kelly. He feigned politeness.

"Sorry, Kenny. Just one beer and you can have your stool back."

Kenny gurgled amiably and leaned on Earl, lest he fall. Then Earl noticed the dog behind the bar and almost backed off his stool. The dog was large enough that it could plant its paws on the bar and look straight into Earl's slightly dilated pupils. Below the bar, beside the dog, was a small brown boy.

"This is Tatum," said the boy. "We rescued him. He's a Great Dane."

"He sure is," said Earl, tentatively scratching the dog under the chin. He looked over his glasses at the boy, A.J.'s son. "Hiya, Jesse."

The evening's company, in the roaring tavern, included Otis and Carol, Teddy Gilbert, the young auxiliary cop whom Otis wanted as a full-time officer, Norbert Klinghofer and his sweetie, Elf Ellefson, and Crystal MacDougal, done up tonight in a lavender batik muumuu and a black Stetson with its brim rolled up Glenn Ford-style. Otis' precocious daughter Natalie had arrived on the bus and was perched on a stool beside her father.

"A kid needs a pet," Crystal said, raising her libation. "But holy Jonah! Maybe not one that's big enough to swallow the kid whole."

Jesse objected, "Tatum wouldn't swallow me."

Carol reached out, got her arm licked up to the elbow, and said, "He's a big baby." She followed this with a burst of baby talk. Natalie stretched across the bar to pet the dog. Tatum responded by trying to climb onto the bar and nuzzle her face. This sent several drinks skidding hither and thither. Kenny, roused reflexively from his torpor, snagged two before they could spill and emptied them before their owners could reclaim them.

A.J. arrived, backed Tatum off the bar, ruffled the dog's ears and attached him to a leash. "Time to go home, Jesse," he said. "Everybody's met your beast."

After a hug from his father, Jesse led Tatum away, Natalie following to the street before returning to her stool.

"I love that big ol' mutt," she said.

"Thank you," said Kenny.

"Chief," said Earl, wrapping his hands around his pint, "I kinda got reamed by the council the other night, over that condemned building down by the bus depot."

Otis sighed. "It seems like all I hear about lately is that place. Wasn't it supposed to be torn down?"

"They used the money on snow removal," said Earl.

"I kinda hate to see it go," said A.J., wiping spilled spirits and dog saliva off the bar. "It's got some history."

"You would know, A.J.," said Crystal, encouragingly.

"Well," said A.J. He turned and cast a glance toward Ernie Olson, the bartender who helped out on weekends. Assured that the trade was under control, he returned to Crystal. "You knew Andy Sturtevant, who ran the S&Q?"

"Well, yes. We were in school together. But he flew south, right?"

"That's right. But he barely left a ripple behind. Just a nice, quiet guy who ran a run-of-the-mill hardware store," said A.J. "Upstairs, though. That's a whole 'nother story."

Crystal nodded knowingly.

"Whaddya mean?" asked Earl.

A.J. leaned his elbows on the bar and waxed sociological. "Y'know," he said. "We say a word like 'ghetto,' and we think big cities. But every little town the size of Hercules, or even smaller, has its slums, where the wretched and lost scratch out their lives. For instance, we got all those families living in trailers and double-wides out at Tornado Estates."

"Tornado Estates?" asked Natalie.

"That's not its real name, Natalie," Carol explained. "But everybody calls it that."

"And then," A.J. continued, "you have all the dark and desolate apartments above the stores and bars along Main Street. That's our ghetto. Single moms whose husbands are just a bad memory. Old folks trying to survive the month on a thousand-dollar Social Security check. Lonesome men who have jobs but drink away their wages or blow it all at the Ho-Chunk casino in the Dells. Families of GIs stationed at McCoy for six months or a year, and then they're gone before their kids can settle into school and make friends. Farm workers without papers who only stay as long as there's a harvest, and then it's 'hasta la vista' before ICE can show up. Sad sacks, addicts, ex-cons, whores, grifters, drifters, cripples and shut-ins ..."

"All the lonely people," said Crystal, "where do they all belong?"

"We don't see much of them, but there they are, living and dying," said A.J. "Upstairs."

A.J. checked on his clientele and got an all-is-well nod from Ernie.

"Course, they weren't all anonymous strangers," said A.J. "When I was growing up, there was this notorious Indian—I mean Indigenous—kid. He was a couple years older than me. Ronny Leaf. Every kid in town was scared shitless of Ronny Leaf, like he was gonna scalp us all and cut out our livers. But all that talk was, what? Urban legend. I can't remember that Ronny ever laid a finger on anyone. Chrissake, he barely *talked* to anyone, and none of us dared talk to him. He was tall and straight as an arrow. Never cracked a smile, never showed any expression at all. I think what was scary was he was just so goddamn dignified. He was sixteen or seventeen, but he carried himself like a sixty-year-old judge who was just about to whack down his gavel and send you to the electric chair. The only time I ever heard him talk was once when I snuck into what used to be Quint Stickles' pool hall. That was the first time I heard Ronny Leaf's voice, and not much of that. He just called the number of the ball and the pocket it was going into. And it went. Every time. I never heard of anybody beating his game."

"Excuse me, A.J.," said Norbert Klinghofer, "what does this Ronny person have to do—"

"With the old Kuckuck building? Well, that's where Ronny Leaf lived, Norbert. He was up there with his mother, in the front apartment. Course, nobody ever saw Ronny's mother. She was called Stella, but I heard that her native name was somethin' like Twilight Star. And she was part of the reason the Kuckuck building got sort of a reputation, Ronny being the scariest Indian brave in the whole county and his mother, Twilight Star, hiding up there in the dark, peeking out the window on Main Street, reciting Gitche Gumee incantations and casting Winnebago spells on the white people passing by on the sidewalk."

"Wow, that's really spooky," said Natalie.

A.J. leaned across the bar and got close to Natalie's face. "Not half as spooky," he said, "as Pyramid Purlew."

"Ooh," said Natalie.

"Purlew," said Crystal. "Why does that name ring a bell?"

"Oh, he was a character, Crys," said A.J. "He lived up there, above the S&Q, for a long time, with his wife—what was her name?"

"Can't help ya," said Crystal.

"Wait, I got it," said A.J. "Elvira, that was her name—like Elvira, mistress of the dark, on TV."

This ancient reference drew a quizzical look from Natalie, Elf and Norbert.

"His name was Francis, actually," continued A.J. "A few people called him Frank, but everybody else called him Pyramid Purlew."

A.J. paused to think and then added a footnote. "He used to drive Cathy Wendorf crazy."

"The librarian?" asked Crystal.

"Yeah, he kept barging into the library and asking for all these obscure books about ancient history. And, well, you know our cute little backwater library. The kind of weird books Purlew wanted, he'd have to go to Madison or Chicago. But that didn't cut it with old Pyramid. He'd go bustin' into the library and raise hell, accusing whoever was at the front desk that they were denying his rights and fostering ignorance 'til one day when Cathy got to the end of her rope and called the police. Well, this drove him out of the library but on the way out, Purlew slams the door so hard that he breaks the glass. He looks up, and there's Big Nate, fresh on the scene with a nightstick and a set of handcuffs."

"Big Nate?" asked Natalie.

"Oh, you didn't know," said A.J. "Nate Neitzel was chief of police before your dad. He died one morning over his breakfast at Calamity's. Roger Steinbeck had to scrape scrambled eggs off Nate's face before he could give him mouth-to-mouth."

A.J. gave everyone a moment to appreciate the tableau.

"Anyway," he proceeded, "I think those were the longest people who ever lived upstairs in the Kuckuck building. Ronny Leaf and his witch-doctor mom up front and Pyramid Purlew in the back apartment. As I recall, Pyramid Purlew stuck it out there 'til after Maye and Faye died. But by then, Elvira was gone. Word was that she just couldn't stand to live any longer with the crazy old fart."

"Well then, A.J., that just leaves one question," said Carol.

"Shoot."

"This Purlew person," said Carol. "Why did people call him—"

"Oops. Hold that thought." A.J. turned. A platoon of GIs had blown into A'Jay's, and they were clamoring for immediate refreshment.

"I'll be back," said A.J., hurrying to Ernie's rescue.

An hour later, he returned and joined in a round of genial ridicule over Otis' masochistic loyalty to the Chicago Bears.

CHAPTER 10

(Monday, the 2nd of June)

Riley had known Analise Grimaldi all his life. They grew up on the same damp block on Minerva Avenue that bordered Emil's Swamp. She was in fifth grade, a year behind Riley. He chose her as his next guinea pig because she was the girl next door. He had never before targeted her for any of his petty cruelties. Judged by grownups, Analise's invitation to the old building would seem to be another case of Riley bullying his peers. But Riley's simmering reservoir of inchoate malice was battling within him, against his curiosity.

He had asked Amy Caruthers what she'd seen, and she only said, "What I was most afraid of, in the whole world." Riley realized that that was how he had felt when he tried to go upstairs and instead plunged into a pit where his father lay dying on a bed of spikes. Ana was as close to being Riley's friend as any kid in town. He didn't want to hurt her, but that building—which didn't want anyone to climb its stairs—had cast a sort of spell. Riley needed to know more.

Ana trusted him.

On a cloudy June day after school, he led her to the crumbling edifice. Riley fed Ana the standard line about some sort of treasure hidden cleverly upstairs and—as usual—he said, "You go first. I'll be right behind you."

Because she was the smallest of all the kids Riley had

guided into the old building, she slipped more easily through the narrow triangle allowed by the tilted door. This time, Riley didn't hang back. He crouched at the doorway, peering inside, trying to discern Ana through a veil of blackness.

For a moment, he could see her blouse, white with tiny blue flowers, but it began to shrink, irising down to a little white circle, then a dot, then nothing. After that pinpoint disappeared, all Riley could perceive was coal-shaft dark and a silence so deep that it roared in his ears.

Ana had seen the stairs as she stepped across the threshold. One step inside and they had vanished. She turned but the door, too, was gone. By turning again, she lost all orientation. She was engulfed in a bleakness blacker than any of the nights that had driven her to hide under her covers. The first touch was not tactile or palpable. It was barely a breath, cold on the back of her neck. Frightened to turn, she spun anyway.

There was nothing, nobody. No thing.

Until it brushed her arm, a velvet fingertip. She looked that way, straining at the inky emptiness. She began to feel again a terror that had followed every minute of her sentient life. The next contact was a hand that, for barely a second—no, not even that long—encircled her wrist, ominously. Disappeared. Ana shivered and held back her voice, not letting it scream, not the way she had cried out the first time she had felt behind her, in the dark, alone ... something. Someone following, waiting, ready to fold her into its arms, lifting her like a baby doll, carrying her somewhere—up? down? she couldn't tell—covering her mouth, squeezing her breath away.

There it was again. She could sense—not feel—a hand, a whole hand, lingering on her back, pressing where she could not reach to swat it away. She twisted 'round, staring so hard into the dark that tears rose in her eyes. They ran hot down her freezing cheeks.

From behind, it took her by both arms. She could feel it now! She could hear it, whispering hoarsely words that made no sense. She twisted in terror. A growing, animal whine mounted in her chest. She knew this thing. She knew what it would do. She had felt it in every nightmare, awakened crying out and trembling. She fought its grip. She knew it would not let go. She knew it was too strong to resist. She didn't want to turn but it turned her. Its hold was now a shroud. It faced her, but as she knew, it had no face. It made its ugly hissing whisper but had no mouth. There was no form. She was alone, alone in the whole world. There was no one, anywhere. Even this thing holding her in a grip whose edges had become sharp, cutting into her skin, growing closer and folding her into itself, was not there. It was nothing. It was just darkness, emptiness. It was solitude so deep and all-encompassing that it would smother her, squeeze out her last breath and carry her—up? down?—into a void deeper than death, like death. But was it death? Would death be kinder than this?

It wasn't just crushing her in its discorporate hold, it was absorbing her. She could feel herself disintegrating, pieces of her falling away and turning into shards of darkness. She tried to suck in a last breath, even for one final scream of desperation, one protest against the horror of her descent into deathless nothing.

Her scream, like a shaft, shattered the darkness. A flood of light struck her in the face and drove Ana back, falling onto the staircase. Mute with fear, she pushed herself up and plunged through a cloud of dust that stung her eyes and tasted on her tongue like iron shavings and spoiled eggs. She crashed into Riley. He staggered back and fell. Ana lost her balance and sank violently to the sidewalk on her knees.

Riley was swiftly upright. He reached down to help Ana to her feet. She recoiled, staring at Riley as though he was the suffocating void that wanted to crush the life from her and send her plummeting—dead? half-dead?—into an eternal loneliness. She struggled her own way up. Her knees were bloody, their pain welcome, a sign of life and air and people in a world she could see and feel. Riley reached out again.

She pushed him away and ran.

Riley watched her go. "Shit," he muttered.

"Ana!" He shouted at the fleeing girl. "What did you ..."

But she was already far away. He knew she wouldn't say. She would never say.

CHAPTER 11

(Tuesday, the 3rd of June)

Carol found herself alone in bed. She looked at the clock on Otis' nightstand. It read just after three o'clock in the morning. She shook her head, rubbed her eyes and got up.

She found Otis poised on the edge of his decrepit recliner, staring at the bottle of Glendalough scotch that occupied the center of a round coffee table in the middle of his living room. The bottle wore a thin layer of dust and a sense of the sacred. Carol paused and regarded Otis.

"You gonna crack the bottle?" she said.

Otis had never joined Alcoholics Anonymous or gone completely off the wagon. But he had long ago forsworn distilled spirits and limited his intake to beer (two pints) among friends at A'Jay's. Since the months-long bender that followed his separation from both the Chicago police and his marriage to Connie, he had only backslid once, drinking himself into violence after an ill-fated reunion with Elena, the poignant street girl who had triggered his flirtation with despair.

"No," said Otis softly, "just window-shopping."

This bottle of rare single-malt was Otis' third. He had shared the first, gingerly, with Carol one night when their tentative relationship had elevated into a palpable passion. The second bottle had gone the way of all booze when a group of friends had invaded his cabin and paid no attention to its symbolic status. On that occasion, Otis hadn't touched the stuff.

The latest bottle had gone unopened—and undusted—for more than a year.

"You couldn't sleep?" asked Carol.

"I guess, yeah."

Carol crossed the room and pushed Otis gently 'til he was sitting back in the old chair. This gave her space to settle into his lap and wrap her arms around his neck. He accepted her there but looked uncomfortable.

"What's the story?" Carol pressed.

Otis finally looked into Carol's eyes. "Okay, I feel like I've failed you."

Carol rolled her eyes. "Oh, come on," she said. "Over this whole marriage thing?"

Otis nodded sheepishly.

"I proposed to you," said Otis, "and then I couldn't bring myself to set a date. I couldn't commit. I don't know what the hell is wrong with—"

"Let me ask you something," said Carol.

"What?"

"In high school, who was your best friend?"

"My *best* friend?"

"Yes, Fosdick, the kid you hung around with after school, cruised the main drag on weekends, talked about girls, smoked your first joint with him, got laid for the first time, and he was the only person you told about it. On graduation day, you were going down to the recruiting office together and join the Marines. Together. *That* kid."

"Well, I didn't—"

"You didn't have a best friend in high school, or in grade school. Did you?"

"I guess."

"You didn't even join the Marines."

"No."

"And when you got onto the police force, you had partners, colleagues, right?"

"Yeah."

"But friends?"

Otis thought this over while Carol stroked his cheek.

"Not really," he said.

"No one who'd come to the hospital if you got shot," Carol prompted.

"Not for sure, no. I mean ..." Otis trailed off.

Carol smiled. "My mother told me once how you can tell a real friend from everyone else."

"Your mother?" Otis was skeptical. "What does she know?"

"More than either of us, Fosdick. Mom's been through the mill."

"Okay, what makes a real friend?"

"Funerals. Hospitals. Moving day," said Carol.

Otis looked puzzled.

"Hard jobs, hard times," said Carol. "A real friend will visit you in the hospital, over and over, and stay there by your bed, no matter how sick, stinky and miserable you are, even if you're dying of cancer or AIDS. A real friend will be at your funeral but they'll also be with you at your mother's and father's funeral and your big brother's funeral. They'll be there when you bury your dog or your pet goldfish. And a real friend will be there to pack boxes and he'll help shlep your furniture in and out of the truck and up six flights of stairs when you move into a new house. A real friend will bring champagne."

"I see," said Otis, uncertainly.

"The biggest change in your life, James Otis, since you moved to this little town in the middle of nowhere, is you've made friends like that, real friends. The first in your life."

"Ya think?" Otis was unconvinced.

"You got shot by Josie Dobbs, remember that?"

"Hard to forget."

"And you spent how many days in the hospital, in Madison—fifty miles away?"

"Um, three."

"And you got visitors, right?"

"Yeah, I did."

"From Hercules, right?"

"Yeah, I did."

"A.J. and Kiayla, right? Crys, Minnie. Earl Schober came twice, right?"

"Well, you were there. And Natalie."

"And those two kids from the Grove, Kratso and his weird sidekick."

"Byron," said Otis.

"All real friends," said Carol, "all of whom will help load the truck when I move in here."

"Oh," said Otis, eyebrows lifted. "You mean?"

"You have a brilliant daughter, who understands why you've always kept your distance, and why you hesitate—until it's too damn late—to leap before you look."

"So?"

"Yes ... roomie."

They kissed.

Otis disengaged and said, "Don't you have a lease on your place?"

"It's up in three months," said Carol. "I'll talk to Dale Gundlach. He's my landlord."

"Well, Dale hardly needs the money."

"Yes, but he didn't get rich by letting people breach their leases. If I have to, I'll leave the place empty and pay the rent 'til it expires."

"Just tell him you're moving in with the chief of police. If he won't let you out of your lease, I'll arrest him."

While Otis was saying this, Carol was removing Otis' threadbare Ron Santo memorial t-shirt, which she had adopted as her nightgown.

Otis assumed an earnest expression. "Listen," he said. "I just want you to know. I'm still gonna marry you."

"Fosdick, I'm naked here. Shut the hell up."

Afterward, they moved to the breakfast bar where, despite the stimulant effect of caffeine, they drank coffee.

"I have a theory," Carol said.

"Has anyone ever suggested that you have too many theories?"

Carol ignored this. "I've concluded that it's part of your nature," she theorized, "to freeze up in the face of big personal decisions."

"I thought I already admitted that," said Otis.

"That's nice. But there's more."

Otis sighed. "Jesus."

"You also have this powerful hangup about unfinished business."

"Oh yeah?" Otis asked cautiously.

"Yes. You remember when Elena lured you away from me. And summoned you up to the Twin Cities, and it turned out she had hooked up with a grifter who—"

"You really don't need to remind me. That was one of my worst—"

"No, that wasn't your worst anything, Fosdick. From the moment you met Elena, you wanted to save her from the rotten life that seemed to be her destiny. You interceded for her. You broke rules. You risked your career and marriage to be her goddamned savior. You helped her over and over again, and every time, she slipped away or just disappeared. You never stopped trying to rescue Elena, and you couldn't give up. She was like an unsolved crime. You needed to close the case."

"And I couldn't."

"And it nags at you, even now. You still wonder where she's gone, what she's doing, what you could—" Carol paused.

She went on, "If the phone rang right now and it was Elena, and she was in terrible trouble—desperate—and she's asking you to come and help her, would you drop everything and go?"

Otis began to say "no," but bit his tongue. His heart sank. "I don't know," he admitted.

"I think you would," said Carol. "I would argue against it. I'd watch you go, and then I'd wait. And when you came back, betrayed and discouraged, I'd turn out to be just as softhearted as you. I would take you back."

"Quietly?"

Carol laughed. "Hardly. You'd be on my shit list for a month."

"A week," countered Otis.

"Two weeks," said Carol, with finality.

"Deal."

They sipped coffee.

"The silver lining, I think, is that Elena is history," said Carol. "Thank God."

Otis waited for the other shoe to hit the floor.

"Which brings us around to Josie Dobbs," said Carol, dropping the shoe. "She's the unfinished business that bugs you and haunts and stalls you from getting on with your life."

Otis pondered this. Josie Dobbs had transformed from a teenage flirt to the most confounding and elusive suspect he had encountered in his career. Even before he had uncovered her role in the robbery of Hercules Hardware, she had used Otis' history with Elena to revive his reputation as a predator of underage girls. While he was losing his job as police chief, she was basking in the town's adulation and heading off to Bryn Mawr.

Driven by demons that Otis couldn't begin to fathom, Josie Dobbs had left a trail of tragedy that had ruined lives and frustrated Otis to the point where he could not get through a day without wondering how and why he had failed to stop her. Josie had fired the bullet that had put him in the hospital. But hardly anyone in Hercules knew about the incident and—if they had been told that the Hercules High Homecoming queen had hunted Otis through the woods, aimed at him through a telescopic sight and shot to kill him—most townspeople would have scoffed at the suggestion that a girl so sweet and charming, kind and wonderful, could bring herself to even swat a mosquito.

Josie was the pride of Hercules and the nemesis of Jim Otis.

"And nobody," said Carol, "has any idea where she's gone. Not even her parents."

"She'll be back," said Otis, with grim certainty.

"I know," Carol agreed. "But you can't put your life on hold waiting for her to pop up."

"You're right. I know," said Otis. He planted a lingering kiss on Carol's lips.

"That's why," Otis continued, lifting Carol from the breakfast bar stool, "I'm putting a whole new chest of drawers in my bedroom and emptying two-thirds of my closet."

Carol grinned. "Baby steps," she said.

"Better than no steps at all," replied Otis.

"Let's go back to bed," said Carol, "and talk about—"

"Josie?"

Carol slapped Otis' ass.

"Moving day," she said.

CHAPTER 12

(Wednesday, the 4th of June)

The Grove was not a place for little boys. Kids as young as Riley Hawkins almost never ventured there. So, when Riley appeared, the regulars viewed him with a suspicion that bordered on hostility. They knew who he was. They figured he'd end up hanging out in the Grove, eventually. But the unwritten rules dictated that the little snot did not belong.

Not yet.

The Grove was a well-trampled patch of bare ground among trees, across the railroad tracks from Calamity Jane's parking lot. In the middle was a makeshift fire pit and several logs worn smooth by a thousand blue jeans. From the age of eight or nine, every boy and girl in Hercules knew where the Grove was and had an idea—usually exaggerated—of what went on there, among those known around town as delinquent, or stoners, punks, losers, sluts and freaks. Many Hercules kids never dared set foot in the Grove. Others, a little more curious and daring, dipped their toes, consorted with the outlaws and took a few bites of forbidden fruit. These were voyeurs, whose only purpose was a stroll on the wild side. They didn't understand the grip the Grove had on its habitués, its burrowers of the village underworld, who sought refuge from homes that had turned into Hell or who lived a transient existence with no home at all. The normies didn't understand the bond among damaged kids that kept them lingering year in and year out in this chill and dreary grotto. The Grove was the shady circle where the angry and bewildered could escape the vicarious aspirations of their parents and teachers, where they could lament among fellow sufferers the troubles that they knew—in their adolescent wisdom—would never end. There was beer in the Grove. There was weed and medication. There was sex and protection from sex. There were whispered plans to plot laboriously and forsake later because they involved too much effort. There was trouble, there was trust.

Most adults steered away from the Grove, pretending it wasn't there, assuming that their children were too nice to ever go there. They kept from their kids their own history in the Grove. Respectable folks often suggested to their police chief, Jim Otis, that he should clear out that place, once and for all.

Otis had grown up in Chicago, where the Grove's equivalent was a street corner, a stoop with magnetic powers, a dark corner in a city park or a puddled underpass where every inch of its walls was spray-painted with tragic salvos against anonymity. Otis had no interest in clearing out the Grove, partly because the task was impossible, mostly because it was a vital source of intelligence. His occasional visits were tolerated because he understood that a cop had no authority there. A kid in trouble was safe in the Grove because of another unwritten rule. If you had real trouble, the kind that violated the sanctuary of the Grove and threatened incursion by authorities higher and crueler than Chief Otis, you couldn't stay.

Otis had watched Riley Hawkins enter the Grove. He was smaller by half than the half-dozen other kids whom Otis knew by name. Somebody had handed the small boy a bottle of beer. Otis watched Riley tip the bottle and gulp at the beer, wincing afterward. The others, all boys except a jittery girl named Jade, who needed at least a month in rehab, were pointedly not talking to Riley.

Otis emerged from the shadows. Everyone looked, then feigned indifference. One kid palmed a joint. Jade glared at Otis, her eyes mixing fear and hatred. Riley froze and stared at the police chief, his body tensed for flight.

Ignoring the others, Otis lied, "Riley, if you run again, this time I'll catch you."

Riley stayed poised to run.

"Ask anyone," said Otis, who had left his cane in the car. He smiled at the group. "I'm old but I'm fast." He nodded toward one boy. "Right, Augie?"

"Shit, yeah, Chief," replied Augie Belzer, who was a sort of elder statesman, age twenty, in the Grove. "You could run me down easy."

Riley, who didn't know about Otis' recently broken leg, took this in.

Otis said, "Riley, you're not in trouble. But I need to talk to you."

"What about?" said Riley.

"I think you know."

"Whyncha jis' leave me alone?"

"Kid." This from Augie Belzer.

Riley turned, surprised to be addressed by one of his elders.

"Get outa here, kid," said Augie. "Talk to the chief, and leave us the fuck alone."

Riley shrank visibly. Otis seized the moment, strode to Riley and guided him away. He caught Augie's eye but got nothing back but the gaze of the iguana.

Riley stayed quiet 'til Otis had led him to his car, a reconditioned Crown Victoria he'd found at a police auction in Rochester. Natalie had nicknamed it the Bluesmobile, after the '74 Dodge Monaco driven by Dan Aykroyd in *The Blues Brothers*.

To prevent his bolting, Otis installed Riley in the passenger seat. He slid in behind the wheel and locked the doors.

"You're trapped," he said.

Riley was defensively sullen, staring at the glove box.

Otis went to the point. "Riley, you know Analise Grimaldi."

Riley reacted to the name but didn't look at Otis. "Yeah. So?"

"So, she hasn't been in school for a couple of days now."

Riley held his ground. "I know that."

"What's worse, she hasn't talked to anyone, not even her mother. Not a word. Nobody knows what's wrong."

Riley stared at the glove box.

"But I think I know," said Otis. He let that sink in. "And I think you do, too."

Riley turned finally, looking up at Otis. He didn't speak.

"I don't think you meant to hurt her," said Otis.

"No," said Riley.

"Word is," said Otis, "she was your friend since you were little."

Riley, eager to agree, said, "Yeah."

They shared a moment of silence. Riley broke it, saying, "Is Ana gonna be okay?"

"Everybody hopes so, Riley. We just have to wait and see."

Otis sank a little, getting his face closer to the boy. "Riley, look, it's my job to take care of this whole town. I have to keep an eye on everything, even when it's just a little girl who won't go back to school and won't tell anyone why."

Riley waited.

"I'm pretty sure you know why."

Riley's eyes lowered.

Otis said, "Riley, I don't think you did anything wrong. Certainly nothing a policeman could do anything about. But Ana's my responsibility. And I think she's yours, too. I just want to know what happened."

Riley looked up, finally exposed. His face was puzzled, penitent, imploring. "It's that place," he said.

"The old Kuckuck building," said Otis.

"Yeah, yeah, S&Q," said Riley. "There's something there. It's like … I don't know … It … It …"

"Are you scared?"

This was a challenge. Riley tensed. His eyes narrowed, his lips went white.

"Tell you the truth," said Otis, "that old wreck of a building scares me. It's spooky. The town's gonna tear it down, eventually. The sooner the better. Meanwhile, there's something going on there, and I have to go inside."

"You're goin' in there?"

"It's my job."

They both thought about this.

"Tell you what. Why don't we go over there now and take a look?"

Riley almost shuddered. "Oh no, not ... um ... not now. No."

"Why not?"

"Um ... it's getting dark. I gotta ..."

It was early evening in June, more than three hours 'til sunset. But Otis didn't argue the point.

"Your mom wants you home?"

"Yeah. Oh yeah."

"Okay then, but how about tomorrow, after school. You've been in there, right?"

Again, a shiver from Riley. "Yeah."

"Good. You probably know that joint better than anybody in town. Will you go with me?"

Riley said, "I don't have to go inside, do I?"

"You don't want to?"

Riley shook his head emphatically.

"But you'll help me?"

"I guess. Yeah."

"After school. I can pick you up."

Riley tightened. "No, I'll ... I'll meet you there."

"Promise?"

"Yeah, okay. Sure."

"If you don't show up, you know I'll have to come looking for you."

"Yeah, I know."

"Good. You want me to drive you home now?"

"No, I got my bike." Riley pointed toward the Grove.

Otis unlocked the car, and Riley clambered out. He waited 'til Riley had mounted his bicycle and headed up Main Street.

Otis pondered the effect of the strange building at the end of town. It had reduced at least one little girl into a catatonic truant and turned a standard-issue grade-school bully into a creature far more complicated—and interesting.

CHAPTER 13

It was Dagwood Night at A'Jay's.

Once a week, A.J.'s wife, Kiayla, made a batch of her renowned Dagwood sandwiches. These multi-story masterpieces featured, among other ingredients, prosciutto, paper-thin tongue, raw onion, Swiss cheese and anchovies. Kiayla stacked all her precisely sliced layers in a particular order, dressed with condiments whose formula had been a family secret for generations, on a light rye bread supplied by a kosher delicatessen in La Crosse. She topped each Dagwood, just before serving, with a layer of her mother's heartbreaking, tear-inducing coleslaw. A.J. and Kiayla brought a stack of Dagwoods to the bar at six sharp every Wednesday. Typically, by 6:45, the huge tray contained only a few shreds of romaine and a faint ambience of Russian dressing.

Carol had arrived at one minute to six, after bailing early from a prolonged faculty meeting at Hercules High. By 6:15, after managing to consume half of a Dagwood, she was blissfully sated. She was dabbing her lips and sipping her second New Zealand sauvignon blanc when Otis limped up to the bar at seven.

"Where's your cane?"

"Doc said I don't need it, as long as I don't try breaking into a dead run."

"You look like it still hurts, Fosdick."

"I can stand it."

"You're my kind of masochist, big fella."

Otis ignored this and caught A.J.'s eye.

"You missed Dagwood night," Carol said. "But I saved you some."

"Thanks. Yeah, I got busy," said Otis. "Hi, Kiayla."

"H'lo, James." Both Kiayla and Jesse were behind the bar. Tatum, the dog, in violation of rules long since codified by the Hercules health board, was there, too. Tatum, drooling subtly in honor of Carol's uneaten portion, had his chin on the bar, close enough for Kenny to dreamily scratch behind an ear.

"Good boy, good boy," chanted Kenny, who was four vodkas deep into his evening blur.

Otis greeted Jesse, who waved and then joined with Kenny in fondling the giant dog. A.J. squeezed past the boy and dog, delivering to Otis a pint of an IPA called Snake Hollow.

"Sorry, James," said A.J. "No Harp."

"No problem." Whenever A.J. was able to acquire a keg of Harp lager, he matched it with a domestic stout and served Otis black and tans.

Over the next half-hour, the end-of-the-bar crowd added Hap Schaller, Teddy Gilbert, who had just handed over the night-shift patrol to Maury Higginson. Making a rare appearance, Minnie Trout ambled in and got a wry smile from A.J. by ordering a Dubonnet. Crystal MacDougal made her entrance in a floor-length blue embroidered Mexican gown with a smocked waist and ruffled three-quarter sleeves. Her shoes were matching patent-leather blue huaraches, and her sombrero had a short brim and a rattlesnake hatband that drew a tentative growl from Tatum.

Having done her duty, Kiayla tucked the big tray under her arm, kissed A.J. farewell and led Jesse out of the bar. The big dog padded along behind. No one got in his way.

Carol greeted a refill of her wine and turned on Otis. "So, you didn't tell me why you were late."

"Late?"

"We were meeting here around six."

"Oh, that's right," said Otis, taking a bite of his half-Dagwood. Coleslaw juice invaded his Tom Selleck mustache. "I was just ... checking something out."

Carol handed him a napkin. "Checking out what?"

Otis had no recourse but revelation. "Well, I was talking with that kid, Riley Hawkins. And—"

"So was I, today. No, I mean, I was talking *about* Riley with Amy Caruthers," said Carol.

"Who?" asked Crystal.

"Amy's in sixth grade," said Carol.

"Sixth grade?" asked Hap. "I thought you taught high school."

"I still do, but I get around, Hap," said Carol. She added, "It's a long story."

A.J. was near. "Ah, long stories are what bars are for. They're half the reason I opened this place."

"Whut's th'other half," asked Kenny blearily. A.J. let this pass.

Carol took a sip and said, "Okay." She explained that one of her students, Maddy Grimaldi, had been distracted in class for several days. That morning, Carol had stopped Maddy after class and asked if something was troubling her.

Carol said, "Maddy was worried about her little sister, Analise, who had stopped talking, wouldn't eat and was afraid to leave her room, much less go to school. All Maddy could get from Ana was that Riley Hawkins had taken her someplace that scared the wits out of her."

"Riley Hawkins," said Minnie. "That figures."

"Maddy gave me the impression that this wasn't an isolated incident. Riley somehow had this effect on other kids, too," said Carol. "So, I asked around the teachers' lounge, hooked into the grapevine and got another name."

"Amy Caruthers," said Crystal.

"That's right."

"I know her mother, Linda. She and I went door-to-door for Tammy Baldwin in the last election," said Crystal.

"Good for you, Crys," said Minnie, politically.

"To Tammy Budwun!" said Kenny, raising his empty glass and hoping for a refill. A.J. ignored him.

"Well, I didn't have a last-period class," Carol went on. "So, I went over to the middle school and managed to track Amy down."

"Wha'd she say?" asked Teddy.

"She said Riley Hawkins ... hm." Carol considered her word choice. "Apparently, Riley lured Amy over to that condemned building up by the bus depot."

"The Kuckuck building," said Minnie, informatively. "Last tenant in there was Andy Sturtevant. S&Q Hardware."

"Thanks, Minnie," said Carol. She paused to gather her thoughts.

"Not to mention the Purlews and the Indians," added Minnie.

"Thanks again," said Carol.

"C'mon. What then?" Hap insisted.

"Well, then Riley convinced Amy to go inside," said Carol. "He handed her some line about a hidden treasure upstairs."

"Oh, come on," said Teddy. "Who would believe that?"

"I don't think she did," agreed Carol. "But she was curious."

"Wait. I thought that old building was locked up," said Hap.

"It was," said Otis. "But the door is broken. It's hanging by a hinge. There's room to squeeze inside, especially if you're small."

"Hey, get real. Even if it was still locked tight," said Teddy, "if kids want to get inside, they'll figure out a way."

"Yeah," said Hap. "I remember."

"So," Carol resumed. "Amy went inside but never got to the stairs. Something happened to her, something terrible."

"What? Riley Hawkins attacked her?" said Minnie, with a sniff of indignation.

"No, no. Amy said Riley stayed outside. She realized afterward that he was probably afraid to go in."

"Riley Hawkins afraid?" said Minnie dubiously.

"So, what happened to the girl?" asked Crystal.

"She couldn't tell me. She was just shivering and pale. She only said that, when she started toward those stairs, in the dark, she saw—or felt—the thing she was most afraid of, in the whole world."

"What? You mean, like," said Hap, "it's haunted?"

"Oh, come on. Not again," muttered Otis. He had spent much of the previous winter coping with the restless spirit of a long-dead basketball hero, John Roszak, who purportedly haunted the Hercules High School gym. The incident had shaken Otis' disbelief in the existence of ghosts.

"No, not haunted," said Carol with a disturbing note of certainty. "Cursed."

"Cursed?" said A.J. "What? By the old-maid Kuckuck sisters? Poor Amy will never get married."

Carol was not amused. "I don't know, but Amy ..." She paused again. "Look, this is a really bright girl. She expresses herself well. She's brave. But she couldn't explain what happened there. She was terrified just trying to remember—no, she was trying to forget. She encountered something sinister, something ..." She hesitated to utter the word. "... diabolical."

"Oh God," said Minnie.

Otis broke in. "Whatever happened to the girl," he said, "happened to Riley, too. It happened to him first."

"Sure. That's why the little bully took other kids there," said Minnie. "To scare the wits out of them."

"Partly, yes. But I think it's not so simple, Minnie," said Carol. "At first, I thought Riley was just being mean, terrifying kids for the fun of it. Maybe for spite."

"Well, he's an angry kid," said Otis.

Carol went on. "But the last thing Riley said to Amy was, 'What did you see?' I think the kids he took there were like lab rats. Something had happened to him, and he couldn't figure it out. So, he experimented."

This left everyone silent for a moment. Otis took the opportunity.

"After I saw Riley today," said Otis, "I was curious. So, I drove over to his house, out on Minerva. It's the last house before the dead end, the only house on the other side of the river. It backs up to Emil's Swamp. I just sat there in the car and looked it over. The place doesn't look like it was meant to be a house at all, more of a barn or a storage shed, like one of those Hooverville shacks from the Depression. No paint, falling apart, sitting on the edge of the swamp, probably infested with mosquitoes. The boy has it rough."

Minnie interceded. "His mother, Beth Ann, she was a Kiefer before she was married. Nice girl, nice parents but they both died before she finished school. Dirt poor but she had, well, dignity. Then, along came Jerry, her drunken rat-bastard of a husband. God knows why women ... well, anyway, the prick half-crippled Beth and then left her in the lurch with that boy to raise. And then she got MS—the on-again, off-again kind. And when it's off, she works at the recycling center over in Cashton, sorting out rubbish and getting her hands all cut up. That poor thing, and now it looks like her little boy is turning out to be just as much of a bastard as his old man ... and good riddance to him. If Jerry Hawkins ever shows his face around here again, I'm gonna send you out to shoot him down in the street, Jimmy."

Minnie took a deep breath.

"So," said Otis, "no sympathy for the mean-streets kid from the wrong side of the river, with his grandparents dead, no dad and a sick mother?"

Minnie lowered her chin and glared through her eyebrows. "Not from me, Jimmy. The brat's a bad seed."

Otis decided not to reveal that he had scheduled a rendezvous the next day with Riley Hawkins at the Kuckuck building. The boy probably wouldn't show up anyway.

CHAPTER 14

(Thursday, the 5th of June)

Otis was mildly surprised to find Riley waiting for him at the doorway of the Kuckuck building. The boy emanated a faint proprietary air, as though he had staked claim on the brick derelict.

"I ain't goin' in there," he said. Otis stopped and regarded Riley.

"I know. We agreed on that," said Otis. "Anything I should know before I cross the threshold?"

Riley's face went through a series of swift changes from confusion to fear to bravado. "Nah," he said finally. "Jist, um ... be careful. Y'know?"

"Okay, *careful* is the word."

These were empty words. Otis expected nothing untoward as he bent to squeeze through the child-size opening and pushed the door farther open. Stepping through and straightening, he heard the heavy oak door creak, closing to its original position behind him.

Darkness swallowed him.

Otis waited for his eyes to adjust, peering into the gloom, seeking the staircase. In the weak light that seemed to trickle into his vision like sap seeping from treebark, he saw no stairs. Suddenly, bewilderingly, he faced—inches away—a ragged wall of rock. He looked upward through gray air at a tower of sandstone and gravel.

The wall's surface crawled and writhed like water on glass. Pits in the rock were gaping mouths that vomited knife-edged shards aimed at his eyes, cutting his face. Through a shower of stinging dirt, he lunged upward, clawing for a fingerhold on the fringe of red roots that trailed, like shreds of flesh, between the spikes and thorns that toothed the treacherous wall. He felt the ground beneath him disappear, his feet suddenly treading on emptiness. He snagged one of the thin tendrils. He was too heavy. Ripping his hands into shredded meat, he clawed for another strand as he felt his only lifeline stretch and fray against the jagged cliff face. He dared to look down at dead trees clustered together, limbs like upstretched talons, mounted on rocks that jutted and gaped like mouths full of broken fangs. Otis looked back up at the root, too weak, too slippery to hold him there.

Otis knew this terror. Forgetting the tenuous strand, his torn fingers and the certainty of death a hundred feet below, he closed his eyes tight. He stilled his struggle. He did not twist and clamber for a grip on the brittle stone. Willfully blind, he hung motionless, heedless to the slipping of his hands, the tension of the root pulling free. He shut his mind from falling, falling, reliving the greatest fear he had ever felt. The closest he had ever come to that childhood horror was a night in college, when a joint spiked with some substance far stronger than mere cannabis had thrown him stumbling toward an imagined wall, where a towering window drew him like a crystal seductress and lured him toward a star-speckled blackness beyond. He had closed his eyes then, as he had crashed through the window and felt himself not in birdlike flight but plummeting toward the blunt force of concrete and a body instantly rendered into broken bone, clots of gore and a pool of jellied blood. He had held his breath, felt the force of his fall tearing at his skin and distending his face. On the brink of impact, a panic that had lasted less than a minute, maybe just seconds, the terror passed. He opened his eyes then not to feet of strangers surrounding his shattered corpse, but to his white and stricken reflection in a bathroom mirror.

Now, the panic fading, he opened his eyes, his hands hanging loose at his side. He clung to no crumbling cliffside. Instead, in weak, yellow light from somewhere above, he saw the ascending lines that marked the staircase. He felt the void in his lungs from forgetting to breathe, and he sucked in air that tasted of soot and decay.

Otis coughed. Feeling for the wall, he turned and saw the triangle of sunlight formed by the tilted door. Stumbling on the doorsill, he stepped outside. Hit by the light, he sneezed once. He looked down. There, almost touching him, Riley looked up. He was taut with anticipation, his eyes wide.

"Wha'd ya see?"

Otis sneezed again.

CHAPTER 15

“You didn’t go *upstairs*?”

A.J.’s question was more like an accusation.

Kenny compounded the indictment, “Jeez, Chief, ya chickened out?”

Otis sipped his pint and smiled dolefully. “I don’t understand, really, but for an instant I was reliving the most frightening moment of my life, and all I could do was back off and get away. You’re right, Kenny. I chickened out.”

“The most frightening of your life,” said Carol. “The night you proposed to me, right?”

“Funny,” muttered Otis.

“Seriously,” said Carol, patting Otis’ hand.

Otis thought for a moment. “My dad, before he died, tried to get me out of the city once in a while. Fresh air, blue skies, all of that.”

He paused.

“Yeah?” said Hap.

“Well, we drove from Chicago to the Mississippi. I was six or seven. I had no idea where I was. But my dad had me hiking along this ridge beside the river. It seemed to me like we were a thousand feet up. I was scared. The trail was narrow. In places, it couldn’t’ve been a foot wide. I looked down and saw that we were ten, twelve yards in from the water. Rocks and dead trees right under me.”

Otis took a breath.

"And?" prompted Hap.

"And I slipped. I started falling. I grabbed these skinny roots sticking out of the rock face. But they tore right out. I knew I was going to die."

Another pause.

"Until?" said Carol.

"Well, my dad grabbed my arm and set me back on the path. He said, 'Careful, Jimmy. Watch your step.'"

Otis stopped.

"That's it? You slipped?" scoffed Hap.

"No." Carol intervened. "He was a little boy. He was old enough to know about death. To think about it. About ceasing to exist, to be snatched from life without warning, into an unknown too horrible to imagine. So, when little Jimmy slipped, here was the abstract come to life, the boy's first actual encounter with death. That moment brought into sudden reality every fear, every monster, every descent into the burning pit, or the swirling maelstrom, or the mouths of the sharks tearing him to shreds that Jim had pictured in his worst nightmares."

"Wow," said Crystal.

"Really?" asked Otis. "I had no idea."

"Just a theory," said Carol with an affectionate grin. She tipped her glass.

"So, you're going back, aren't you?" said Crystal. "To face your worst nightmare?"

"To the Mississippi River?" asked Otis.

Crystal scowled. "To the Kuckuck building, smartass."

Otis shrugged. "Well, I suppose ..."

"Ya have t'go back," said Maury. "It's your duty, as an officer of the law."

"And the guardian of the community," said Crystal.

"That, too," said Maury.

"That old building is a goddamn mystery," said Hap. "If the

chief of police can't solve a mystery—"

A.J. broke in. "Carol, you said the place was cursed."

"As a figure of speech, A.J.," Carol replied. "Not a rational conviction."

A.J. shook his head and leaned close. "The point of a curse, babe, is that it's not rational."

"If it's a cursed building," mused Crystal, "who cursed it?"

"The Indians done it," muttered Kenny.

"Indians?" said Hap.

"Wait. Kenny might be on to something," said A.J., rewarding Kenny's flash of clarity with a refill. "Remember, I told you about Ronny Leaf, the Ho-Chunk kid, and his mother?"

"Stella," said Otis.

"Otherwise known as Twilight Star," said Crystal, who this evening was channeling Dale Evans in a fringed buckskin dress dyed a muted lavender and cinched with a turquoise-studded belt. She wore a cowgirl Stetson and a bandanna neckerchief.

A.J. said, "Our local legend had Stella Leaf as a sort of Indian priestess."

"You mean witch doctor," said Hap, who hitched up his belt and clanked disruptively. Hap had never been seen without the tools of his trade arrayed on his waist and threatening to pull down his pants. It was rumored that he wore his toolbelt to bed.

"The correct term," said Carol in her schoolteacher voice, "is shaman, a spiritual leader and healer. Most native tribes used to practice some sort of shamanism."

"Like a priest?" said Maury.

"Well then, this woman, what's her name again?" asked Hap.

"Stella," said A.J. "Twilight Star."

"I thought the Indians had rules against women being chiefs and shamans and all that," said Hap. "Weren't they just s'posed to stay in the wigwam, crack corn and make papooses?"

"That's actually a good question, Hap," said Carol. "Could a woman be a shaman?"

Silence descended.

"Shit, what do we know?" said Maury. "We gotta ask an Indian."

They looked at one another.

Finally, Crystal said, "Angie?"

"Oh, Jesus," said Otis.

"Call 'er up," Hap demanded. He tapped Otis' mobile phone, lying quietly on the bar beside his beer.

"Tonight?" asked Otis.

"The iron," said Carol, "is hot, Fosdick. Two hours ago, you chickened out of a building which, for all we know, was defended by the curse of a Ho-Chunk witch."

"Oh, c'mon."

"Call 'er up," Hap repeated.

"Don't be chicken," said Kenny.

"Jesus."

A dozen eyes bored Otis expectantly.

"What if she's already in bed?"

"It's 8:30," said A.J. "Nobody's in bed at 8:30."

"Call 'er up."

Otis had dealt with Ho-Chunk activist Angelina Killdeer several times before, most intrusively during the abduction of Carrie Crowfoot. Angie had been more hindrance than help. Her number was stored in his phone.

She answered after four rings. Otis identified himself and put his phone on speaker.

"I know who it is," Angie snapped. "What the hell do you want?"

Otis tried to sound soothing. "Angie, hi. Listen, I'm over at A'Jay's. A few of us were talking, and the subject of Ho-Chunk customs came up. And frankly, I can't think of anyone who knows more—"

"Are you actually tryin' to butter me up, Otis? Don't even think about it. I was just getting ready for bed."

"At 8:30?" said Kenny.

"Who the hell was that?" asked Angie.

"Never mind that. Look, I just have a question."

"About Ho-Chunk customs? I don't believe it. You don't give a shit—"

"No, it's true. We're really interested."

"We?" asked Angie suspiciously.

"Yes," said Otis. "There are several of us here. As soon as the question came up, everybody said, 'Call Angie. She'll know.'"

Angie didn't respond. Otis waited.

Finally, "Well, ask your goddamn question, kimo sabe."

"Okay, Angie. I was wondering if you remember a woman, a while back, named Stella Leaf."

"Stella Leaf?" Angie paused. "Yes, I've heard of her. Her people called her Twilight Star."

"We're hoping you might be able to tell us about—"

Angie's tone changed suddenly. "You're over at A'Jay's?"

"Yes," said Otis.

"Stay put. I'll be right over," said Angie. "Order me a vodka martini."

"Shaken, not stirred?"

Angie snorted and hung up.

Angelina Killdeer reached A'Jay's fifteen minutes later. She was in her usual uniform of flannels and jeans. Her single gray-black braid, which had been growing since she was a teenager, was piled in an unruly bun atop her head and secured with a criss-cross crown of hatpins. She elbowed up to the bar, toppled Kenny onto the floor and drank down half her martini before speaking.

"I'm not payin' for this," she said to Otis. "Or the refill."

Otis nodded.

Angie spoke.

"Most people don't remember," she said. "But there was a Ho-Chunk community south of here, in an oxbow on Jug Creek. They were just a few families livin' hand to mouth. The leader was a man they called Sun Through Leaves. He tried to keep up the old ways, but the old folks all died off and the young ones drifted away, all except for one, Sun Through Leaves' youngest son."

"That would've been Ronny Leaf?" A.J. guessed.

Angie scowled at the interruption.

"Sun Through Leaves was in his sixties when the Jug Creek tribe shrank to just him, his wife and the boy. Without any help to hunt and fish and raise crops, they couldn't live off the land and woods any longer. The winters must've been sheer hell. So, they ended up settling in Hercules. The town clerk, I think it was Madge Mellusi then, she registered Sun Through Leaves' family as the Leafs. Folks got to calling the old man Sunny. His wife, Twilight Star, got listed on the street list as Stella. Ronnie might've had a Ho-Chunk name, but he never used it, and there weren't any Jug Creek Ho-Chunks left to remember it."

Carol said, "Okay, Angie, so while the Jug Creek community was still active, the father, Sun Through Leaves, was the group's patriarch, right?"

"Probably."

"So, the question is, was Sun Through Leaves also a shaman?" asked Carol.

"That's hard to say," Angie admitted. "From what I've heard, Sunny stuck with as many of the old customs as he could, even when the family settled here. He only talked to white people when he had to. I was told by one of my elders that he always looked angry. I know how he felt."

"So," said Crystal, "Sunny wasn't particularly sunny."

Angie almost smiled. "Once when I was little, my mother pointed him out to me. It was just a passing glance, but it stuck in my mind, because he was the spookiest old brave I ever saw. He was like a walking symbol of all the misery dumped on us—the original Americans—ever since that motherfucker Columbus."

"So," said A.J., "you knew him."

"Not at all. I was just a tyke when he died. My grandparents called him a holy man. They talked about how he could heal the sick and read minds and talk to the dead spirits. There was a legend that he could move things without touching them. If I'd seen him do that, I think I would've run away screaming."

"Sounds like a shaman to me," said Crystal.

"What about the wife? Was she a witch doctor?" asked Hap.

"Witch doctor?" Angie waved her empty glass. A.J. responded by filling it. "Ho-Chunk don't have witch doctors."

"Oh. Sorry," said Hap.

"Sunny saw the handwriting, though," said Angie. "Our traditions were dying, and he knew they'd all be gone when he was gone. Ronnie didn't care about any of that. The kid couldn't speak Hoocąk. If Sunny had any hope of passing on his knowledge of the spirit world before he died, his only choice was Twilight Star."

"I see. But she was a woman," said Crystal. "Women weren't allowed—"

"Traditionally, yeah," said Angie. "But she was the end of the line."

"Any port in a genocide," said Crystal.

"Ya got that right," said Angie.

"Okay, so, if we deduce that old Sun Through Leaves taught some of his tricks to his wife, that would make Twilight Star the last of the Ho-Chunk shamans," said A.J.

Angie shook her head. She scanned the faces around her. "All right, look," she said. "I never met Star. I never even saw her. She was up there, in that dark apartment, looking out the window. She never came out. People walked by—white people—they could see her peeking down between the curtains, staring at 'em, no expression on her face. She was scary, but that was easy. You people are all afraid of us. Still think we're gonna put on war paint, sneak into your cabin in the dark and brain you with a tomahawk, take your scalp and steal your kids."

"Angie, we do not think that," Crystal protested. "You know better."

Angie glowered.

"Angie, I called because we wanted to know if Stella had any ... powers," Otis prompted.

Angie relented. "Powers? No, I don't think so. Crys was right in the first place. Sunny was too old and mean and stuck in his ways to share his secrets with a woman, even his wife. But that didn't stop people from talking when they saw her starin' down from that window like Geronimo's twin sister. I guess you could say the old lady got promoted to witch doctor by popular demand."

"Plus," said Carol, "the association with her husband."

"Right," said Crystal. "The apple doesn't fall far from the shaman."

"Awright, so we don't know one way or t'other," said Hap. "Old Sunny might have taught his wife how to cast Ho-Chunk spells, or he might not."

"Probably not," said A.J.

"He didn't," insisted Angie.

"Yeah, fine. But just for the hell of it, let's say he did," Hap said. "Could she have put a curse on a building?"

Angie fingered the fine black hairs on her chin. "You mean," she said, "was she the loneliest old squaw in town, watching life pass by? Did she feel like that dark apartment in that crumbling building was a prison? Did she grow a little more bitter every day?"

Angie paused long enough to receive a third martini. "You have to remember, Twilight Star had lived most of her life outdoors, summer and winter. When the family first came to Hercules, they rented a house, such as it was, down by the river, 'til they were flooded out in that wet spring forty-some years ago. Sunny was already dead then, and all Twilight Star could afford was that dingy hole up above the hardware store. No sun, no breeze, no light. She was alone there, day in and day out. Ronnie came and went, but never stayed. If he didn't bring food or cook for her, she went hungry. She could barely walk, and those stairs? If she even set foot on 'em, she'd end up dead or dying at the bottom. Nobody would know. She could've laid there for a week, 'til Ronnie came home and found her. So, yeah ..."

Angie drank down her martini. "... If Stella had it in her power to put a curse on anything, it would've been on that fucking dark hellhole of a building, where she died. Alone."

Nobody spoke for a while. A.J. poured Angie another drink.

"So, you being Ho-Chunk," said Crystal, carefully, "if you were to go over there, to that building, could you tell if there's a curse on it?"

Angie snorted. "Politics is my calling, Crys. Fighting for Indigenous rights, getting support to fight substance abuse, trying to keep Ho-Chunk kids in school. Do you have any idea how much of the farmland around here rightfully belongs to the Ho-Chunk? It was stolen from us. Ripped off."

"You're not the spiritual type, then?" offered Carol.

Angie smiled at that and clinked glasses.

After a moment, Angie cocked her head. "But, y'know, there is someone who might be."

"Spiritual?"

"Yeah."

"Who?"

Everyone waited.

"John Stormwalker," she said.

Maury recognized the name and sputtered with disbelief. "Old John? That broken-down stoner? Jesus, Chief, how many times have we arrested that guy?"

"Not exactly arrested, Maury," replied Otis. "We've put him up in one of our cells a few times, when he wasn't quite up to finding his way home."

"And then we had to fumigate the damn cell afterwards," groused Maury.

"Doesn't he live out beyond Emil's Swamp, in a sort of ... is it a teepee?" asked Crystal.

"John calls it a cliporoke, which is a Hoocąk word that would mean wigwam or wickiup," said Angie. "It's really just a shack that he put together with whatever materials he could find."

"Yeah, well, he smokes a lot of dope," said Maury indignantly.

After four vodka martinis, Angie had mellowed. She set Maury straight. "What he smokes, Maury, isn't what you white folks call dope. His formula goes back generations. There's a kind of hemp that grows around here, but it has a really low THC content. John's mixes it with herbs, grasses, fungi, wild tobacco, tree sap, dried chipmunk scat, other stuff that's secret, all mixed together in a sort of shaman's cigar. According to him, if you smoke one of John's joints and your heart is pure, you'll pass into a trance that takes you into the Upper World where you can speak with the spirits of the Weyekins."

"What's a Weyekin?" asked Hap.

"Well, it's your great-grandmother," said Angie. "It's Abe Lincoln and Martin Luther King. It's Sitting Bull."

"The spirits of the dead," said Carol.

"So, besides being a fallin'-down doper who never takes a bath," said Maury, dripping with skepticism, "this John Stormcloud is, like, a witch doctor?"

"We don't have witch doctors," Angie repeated. "And I wouldn't call John Stormwalker a shaman. But he's the closest thing this town's ever gonna see."

She had a second thought and addressed it to Carol. "I don't think he talks to the dead, but the Ho-Chunk around here respect him as a sort of a prophet. He's called Stormwalker because when he was just a baby, he crawled out of his house. It was cold and raining and he was naked, but he pushed his way outside, got up on his little feet and starting climbing the hill behind the house. When his parents realized he was missing, they rushed outside looking for him and saw him scrabbling up the hill. As they chased him, the river swelled into a flood and washed their home away. John seems to know when someone is about to fall ill. He sees death before it happens. He has a kind of radar for bad vibes."

"So, if Stella Leaf put a curse on the Kuckuck building, John Stormwalker's the one who could sniff it out?" asked Crystal.

"That's the current barroom theory," said Angie, looking around the bar. "But I wouldn't make book on it. More likely the building wasn't cursed by redskins—or anybody else—and you white folks are just looking for monsters under the bed."

"You're probably right, Angie," said Otis. "But there's something going on there. When I tried to go inside, something stopped me. Something powerful that I can't describe. I've never been so scared in my life."

"So, right now," said Carol, "we still think that maybe Twilight Star exacted revenge for all the insults and injuries of her Indigenous lifetime and cast an evil spell on anyone who tries to enter the building where she died with no one to hold her hand and no ear to hear her last words."

Angie held up a hand, passing on A.J.'s offer of a fifth martini. "Tell you what," she said. "I'll drop in on John tomorrow. We'll share a reefer, catch up on tribal gossip and I'll see if he feels like coming into town to exorcise Ho-Chunk goblins from an empty hardware store."

CHAPTER 16

(Friday, the 6th of June)

Otis got the call from Angelina Killdeer the next morning. She told him she had never seen John Stormwalker quite as animated as he was when she revealed the weird goings-on in Twilight Star's former dwelling.

"He said he's always had a feeling about that place. He didn't think Stella was the sort of girl who'd go quietly to the Happy Hunting Ground."

Otis said, "Do you really call it the Happy Hunting Ground?"

Angie sniffed, "I'm translating, white eyes."

She hung up.

"Well, well, well," said Minnie, who had been eavesdropping. "The plot thickens."

"Minnie, please. You have to keep this quiet," said Otis. "I don't want a crowd."

"Mum's the word," replied Minnie. "But I wouldn't miss this one for all the penguins in Greenland."

Shortly after four o'clock that afternoon, Otis, accompanied by Minnie, arrived at the Kuckuck building. He had come with a pocketful of tools.

"Keep an eye out," he said to Minnie.

"For what?" Minnie replied.

Otis didn't answer. He started working with a heavy-duty screwdriver on the door hinges. The bottom hinge had broken from the frame, causing the door to tilt. The challenge was to remove the upper hinge. The screws were frozen in place and wouldn't budge.

"I should've brought a hatchet," said Otis. "The wood's half-rotten."

"Interesting, Jimmy," said Minnie. "Too bad the hardware store went out of business."

Otis continued to struggle. After a moment, a third voice said, "Whatcha doin'?"

Otis paused his labor and looked down. "Riley, what are you doing here?"

"I figured you'd be back today, bro."

Otis stifled the urge to scold the boy. It was pointless. Riley was the least likely kid in Hercules to shrink in the face of grownup censure.

After watching Otis for a while, Riley had some advice. "It'd be easier if ya jist pull it off."

Breathing hard and sweating, his arm muscles strained and aching, Otis backed up and studied the door. He spied a vertical crack between the flakes of ancient paint on the frame. "You might be right, Riley."

Otis took a position on the knob side of the door.

"Give me a hand?" he asked Riley.

The boy leapt to the task. As they pulled, Otis rocked the door. The crack in the frame widened. With a crunch and a sharp snap, the door broke away, taking with it the hinge and a top-to-bottom strip of frame. Otis staggered backward, almost falling beneath the door. Minnie caught Riley before he hit the sidewalk. The heavy old door teetered and toppled, clattering on the sidewalk in a puff of acrid dust.

Otis caught his breath while peering into a doorway that was still wreathed in deep shadow. Before his eyes could adjust, he realized he had more company than Minnie and Riley. He turned and found Angelina at his elbow. She squinted into the dark rectangle.

"Don't look cursed t'me," she growled.

"Where's Stormwalker?" Otis asked.

Angie leaned her head down the street, where a hunched figure was closing a car door. "He moves a little slow," she said.

John Stormwalker advanced in a scraping shuffle. Over a red thermal long-sleeve with a henley collar, he wore a pair of OshKosh B'Goshes so often washed that they were more white than blue. Over his shoulders was an incongruously bright granny-square shawl mottled with brown stains. He wore a muslin headband bearing the logo of a rice distributor. His braid, ink-black despite age, trailed down his back. Otis looked down and noticed that the old Ho-Chunk was wearing two-tone bowling shoes, orange and blue. As Stormwalker got closer, Otis picked up an aroma that hinted at cannabis and cumin.

"*Aho*," said Otis, whose one word in Hoocąk was "hello."

Stormwalker lifted his face laboriously, looked into Otis' eyes and said, "Been a while, Chief."

"You look like you're doing well."

"Horseshit," replied Stormwalker, his lip curling ironically.

Otis and Stormwalker faced each other on the Main Street sidewalk, the old Ho-Chunk standing only as tall as Otis' collar button. The amenities were finished.

Otis said, "Angie told me that you're sort of a shaman."

"I ain't."

Otis pressed. "But you come from a long line of shamans, don't you?"

Stormwalker seemed to ponder this accusation.

"My old man," Stormwalker finally said, deliberately, "could look a black bear in the eye. Put it right out. Cut the bear's throat while it was sleeping."

"Wow," said Riley.

"I can't do that," said Stormwalker with a wry smile. "Scared shitless of bears. Raccoons, too. Little fuckers got rabies."

"John, I told ya," said Angie, getting down to business. "There might be a curse on that old building."

"That would be ol' Twilight's doin'," said Stormwalker softly.

"That's what we think," said Angie.

Stormwalker nodded. "I guess if any old Injun could call down the wrath of God, it was Stella."

The small group fell silent. Cars passed. "Well," said Minnie.

Stormwalker held up a finger, then rooted in a pocket of his overalls, extracting a hip flask.

"What's that?" asked Riley.

With a note of awed reverence, Angie said, "It's the black juice."

"What's in it?" pressed Riley.

"Hush, you," said Minnie.

With stiff fingers, Stormwalker unscrewed the cap, lifted the flask and gulped a mouthful of its contents. The trickle that escaped the corner of his mouth was thick and inky.

Stormwalker took a series of deep breaths, exhaling an odor of rotted leaf litter and black coffee. No one moved until, with a sudden lurch, the old man bent over and vomited, mostly on Otis' shoes.

"Whoa, gross!" said Riley as he backed away.

"He needs that," said Angie, almost in a whisper, "to enter his trance, to cross into the Upper World, to see the Weyekins."

"What's she talkin' about?" asked Riley.

"Hush," said Minnie.

Shoving Otis aside, Stormwalker began to shuffle, bleary-eyed toward the dark doorway. He paused a moment at the sill and leaned backward as though falling. Straightening suddenly, he reached forward, his fingers curled in half-fists. He crossed the threshold.

Stormwalker stood still on the same patch of filthy floor that had plunged Riley into a pit of knives, Amy Caruthers into a drowning pool and Otis into the deepest terror of his childhood.

Tense and mystified, Otis watched. Except for a trembling that seemed to seize his body, Stormwalker remained motionless on the spot. Otis expected that, eventually, the old man would flail in fear and confusion, stumbling back, perhaps collapsing violently onto the pavement. Just in case, Otis moved closer. Two minutes passed, then three and four, which seemed forever. For five minutes, Stormwalker was frozen in place.

He seemed to shudder. He spread his arms and gripped the doorframe, stepping back. He lifted his face to the sky and turned.

"John?" said Angie.

Stormwalker seemed not to hear. He took several short steps and sank to the sidewalk. He tucked his legs and lowered his head.

"Well?" said Minnie, finally.

Angie spun on Minnie with a murderous glare. Minnie, undaunted, scowled back. Angie dropped to the sidewalk and slid close to Stormwalker. She began to speak, soothingly, in a language no one else could understand.

During Stormwalker's performance, a bank of clouds had come over the town. The staircase up into the Kuckuck building, faintly visible after the door had been removed, had receded into darkness and, once more, disappeared. The sky began to spit a light rain. Stormwalker was oblivious. Angie kept whispering.

The rain became a drizzle. Stormwalker, at last, regained a sort of consciousness. He spoke to Angie. She replied. They whispered, inaudibly, incomprehensibly, beneath the patter of raindrops. When Stormwalker was finished, he folded into himself, as though exhausted.

Angie stood, keeping a hand on Stormwalker's limp shoulder.

"He says ..."

"Yeah?" said Minnie.

"I wouldn't've believed it," said Angie.

"Believed *what*?" piped Riley.

Angie addressed Otis. "There is a curse," she said.

Angie breathed deeply, her expression absent its usual truculence.

"But it's not Ho-Chunk," she said.

"It isn't?"

"He felt its power ... its hatred. He heard its voice, but he couldn't understand."

Otis looked down at Stormwalker, still motionless, rain beginning to soak his headband and run down his hair.

"Is that all he said?" he asked Angie.

"Just one other thing."

Otis waited. Angie lowered her voice.

"Remove the body."

"Remove the body?" said Otis.

"Remove the body?" Minnie repeated, louder.

"Remove what body?" said Riley.

"Jesus Christ," said Angie. "Shout it to everybody in town, why don'tcha?"

Otis regarded the old Ho-Chunk "shaman." He cast Angie a glance of exasperation and wiped rain off his face.

"The hell with this shit," he snarled.

Fueled by anger and frustration, Otis charged the doorway of the Kuckuck building. He passed the threshold without hesitation. He was almost across the entry when he felt his feet sink—to the knees—in gummy, clinging water. He could feel something like hundreds of knives, spikes, razors, ripping his clothes, slashing his skin, blood running down his arms, his scalp, his cheeks. The darkness was smothering, like a thread of black wool worming into his mouth, clogging his nostrils. There were hands without flesh touching his neck, wrapping steel fingers around his throat. Between his legs, he felt a rasping tongue and cat's teeth. He knew where the steps were, just in front. He reached, only to grab a handful of slimy roots. Coarse tendrils wrapped his wrists, cutting deep, clinging. Dirt filled his mouth. He spat it out. He tore out the roots, flailed at the cutting blades, reached again, touched the bottom step. He clawed and scrabbled with his feet, his sodden shoes like lead weights. Crawling on his knees over shards of glass, he got a finger onto one step, then another. He rolled, squirmed, swung fists at the black well around him, clambered desperately to his feet. Standing!

He was on the first step.

Free!

Two steps, three at a time, his gunshot thigh throbbing with pain, Otis sprinted upstairs. His fingers brushed both walls as he climbed.

Gasping for breath, Otis stood atop the staircase, still blind in the darkness. He felt for blood on his face. There was none. He felt, instead, raindrops and peered upward. Through a hole in the roof, he saw a gray patch of light. Water speckled his face.

A moment later, a body slammed into Otis' legs, almost knocking him over.

"Sorry, Mr. Cop," said Riley. "I couldn't see ya."

"You followed me?"

"Yeah."

Otis couldn't resist asking. "Riley, what did you see?"

"That's the weird thing, man. Nothin'."

Too weak to be curious, Otis went no farther inside. After a moment, he and Riley descended toward the street into a steady rain. Minnie, who had remembered to bring an umbrella, was waiting on the sidewalk. Carol was sharing the umbrella. Angelina was gone, along with her chastened witch doctor.

As they hurried toward Otis' car, Minnie said, "Well, wherever it came from, Jimmy—I mean, whether it's real or just a bunch of kids scared of their own shadow, it looks like you've lifted the curse."

"No way, man," said Riley. "Not 'til we remove the body."

Carol stopped and looked piercingly at Otis.

"What body?"

CHAPTER 17

(Tuesday, the 10th of June)

No secret survives in a town as small and nosy as Hercules.

Over the weekend, word had gotten out about the strange doings at Faye and Maye Kuckuck's decrepit tenement. On Monday in school, kids descended on Riley Hawkins, demanding details on the monsters and spooks roaming its rooms and bushwhacking intruders. Riley, in his lifetime's first exercise of discretion, heeded Otis' counsel and told no tales.

So, of course, kids made stuff up.

By Tuesday evening, the Kuckuck building was back on the city council agenda. Jim Otis was summoned. Quietly pleased at the ruckus, Carol joined him and waited for his report to come around on the agenda.

Otis' testimony came under "Old Business" after a lengthy discussion about the folks living in the rowhouses in Tech Terrace who persisted in raising chickens and rabbits inside the city limits. Otis, who was disinclined to prevent poor people from raising food to feed their children, once more assured Gloria Osterholm, the council's anti-livestock crusader, that he was "working on" the problem—by attrition.

"What do you mean, 'attrition'?" snapped the councilwoman.

Otis was saved by Chairman Roland Cedarfield. "Enough with the chickens, Gloria," he said, lowering his gavel. "Chief

Otis, I thought we were done with ghosts in Hercules!"

"I don't believe in ghosts, Ron," said Otis, struggling to mask his uncertainty. He had, after all, been a reluctant witness to the hauntings of John Roszak.

"Well, dammit, neither do I!" Cedarfield retorted. "But the whole damn town is shivering in their boots 'cause they think the Kuckuck building is possessed."

"By dead Indians!" said Councilman Charles Luger, with a wink. "On the warpath! Looking for scalps."

"Chuck," interjected Councilwoman Sandra Rendell, "I believe the acceptable term is 'Native Americans.'"

"Nowadays, yeah," replied Luger. "But when these ghosts died, they were still Indians."

"Oh my God."

Wielding his gavel, Cedarfield nipped the digression. He began speaking in a voice that made clear he would brook no interruption. "I got a call the other day from Diana Grimaldi, who said this boy took her daughter Analise ..."

Cedarfield paused, then continued. "Now, this boy, he has a bad reputation. Troublemaker, a juvenile delinquent. But Mrs. Grimaldi said the boy, Riley Hawkins, well, he was a neighbor, sort of a friend of her little girl. So, the woman was upset ... very upset! This wasn't just a dirty trick. It was ... it was a betrayal. This boy, Riley, who she thought she knew, took little Analise over to this condemned building up Main Street and just terrorized her."

Cedarfield gathered his thoughts. No one spoke.

"Now, the girl, little Analise, she didn't say what happened. The poor thing couldn't even talk. She never said a word for almost a week. Her mother took Analise to the doctor, who told her that, thank God, the boy hadn't done anything ... er, sexual. But the little girl was scared shitl—to death. Now, this wasn't the only call I got, or Mayor Winstead. Right, Luke?"

Mayor Luke Winstead, his eyes lowered, nodded uneasily.

Cedarfield kept on rambling. "There were other children

who were lured into that dangerous building by the Hawkins boy. And they were also terrorized and upset. Now, I'm told, well after the fact, that our police chief has somehow colluded with that little ne'er-do-well, that bully, Riley Hawkins, in organizing some sort of Indian powwow at that building. Unless I've been lied to, Chief Otis involved a child, young Riley, with the town's most notorious drug user, John Stormwalker! The chief—admit it, Jim!—went ahead with this weird episode without consulting this council, without even informing Luke, our mayor, who's been dealing with a flood of phone calls from parents about haunted houses and frightened children, and God knows what the *hell* is going on ... Chief!"

Silence reigned in the City Hall.

Twenty long seconds passed before Cedarfield, brandishing his gavel, glared at Jim Otis and said, "Well?"

Otis, who was seated in the second row of plastic seats, uncrossed his legs and leaned slightly forward. "So, Digger," he said, "does this mean I have the floor?"

"Why should we listen to him?" broke in Councilwoman Gloria Osterholm. "That building's been a public hazard for years. We should just order the DPW to go over there and tear it down—tomorrow."

"Gloria," began Cedarfield, "it's not quite as easy—"

"And while we're at it," broke in Councilman Luger, "we should kick that brat out of our schools. Teach 'im a lesson."

Riley Hawkins was present on Otis' suggestion and lurking in the back row. He stood up. "Hey!" he cried.

Cedarfield's gavel came down ringingly. "Order!" he bellowed. *"Order!"*

Order returned, tenuously.

"If we can't tear it down," Councilman Abe Jaffe said, almost too softly to be heard, "wouldn't it be prudent to seal it up ... for the time being?"

Jaffe was one of Otis' allies on the council. Otis stood.

"You're right, Abe," he said. "But before we do that, I need to go back in there."

"Go back?" asked Cedarfield. "The place is a firetrap. It's falling apart. It's condemned. We can't be responsible for you—or anyone—going in there and ... well, what if the floor gives way? What if the roof caves in?"

"If it doesn't kill ya, Chief, the lawsuit could bankrupt the town," said Chuck Luger, a lawyer whose La Crosse practice specialized in personal injury cases.

Ignoring this byplay, Otis began, "I can't explain it exactly."

He didn't want to introduce into this discussion John Stormwalker's cryptic parting utterance.

"But I think there's something about that building that needs to be looked into before we tear it down, or even seal it off."

"What the hell is this man talking about?" muttered Gloria Osterholm.

Otis gripped the chair in front of him. "The boy you're talking about, Riley Hawkins, is here. He was afraid to come, but I told him he had to show his face. He has to be accountable."

"We are not," Cedarfield said, "going to hear from a child, especially one—"

"No, you're not," said Otis. "There've been too many kids traumatized already."

Carol almost giggled.

Otis went on, "Riley discovered something strange in that building. He took other kids there, and they saw, or heard—or felt—something strange there, too. Honestly—well, Ana Grimaldi's mother had it right—they were scared to death. And ..."

Otis raised his eyes. He exhaled audibly. "... so was I."

The council stared at Otis, but no one answered.

"Whatever it is, it affects your mind. It causes frightening visions—nightmares. It might be something simple," said

Otis. "A gas leak or some hazardous substance that nobody knew about."

"My God, what if there's somebody in there cooking crystal meth?" said Luger.

"I doubt that. I know how that smells, Chuck. But we can't rule out anything before we've gone in there," said Otis. "So, I ask the council to hold off on any action on that place, I believe it's called the Kuckuck building."

"That's right," said Abe Jaffe.

"Before you order it torn down," Otis went on, "I need to search it inside and out, top to bottom."

"To find what?" insisted Gloria Osterholm.

"Crystal meth," said Luger.

Otis ignored this. "No idea, Gloria," he admitted. "Probably nothing."

"Nothing?" intoned the councilwoman, "except rotten floors, lead paint, poisonous gas and illegal drugs?"

"And rats, too, I bet," added Luger. "We can't wait! We have to tear down that death trap *now!*"

"Well, then, dammit," said Gloria, "I move that we seal off that building, post it off-limits to everyone including the chief of police, and have the Department of Public Works bulldoze it into a pile of haunted rubble."

"Second that," piped Luger.

The ensuing debate traveled in predictable circles until Luke Winstead intervened and suggested that no harm could come from a cursory once-over of the Kuckuck sisters' legacy before its demolition. Gloria and Chuck manned the minority in a 3–2 vote, after which Chairman Cedarfield ordered that Chief Otis sign a liability waiver before setting foot on the bottom step of the staircase.

"Glad to, Digger," said Otis.

Afterward, as they headed to the car, Carol told Otis that she had caught and talked with Riley Hawkins as he was fleeing the City Hall. "I don't know how you did it, Fosdick. But you shrank the chip on that kid's shoulder."

Otis shrugged. "He's a tough kid. He's angry."

"Yes, but you listened to him. That worked."

"Barely," said Otis. "And how long will it last?"

"I wonder," Carol agreed. "But it would help Riley if you took him along."

"When I search the building?"

"Yes."

"No. Digger was right. That old place is dangerous. What if he gets hurt?"

"What if he spends the rest of his life not trusting anyone?"

Otis rarely won an argument with Carol.

"Shit."

CHAPTER 18

Angelina Killdeer was waiting for Otis at A'Jay's. She was using his stool and luxuriating in a margarita. "I thought you'd never get here."

"That's my barstool."

"I didn't see your name on it, kimo sabe."

A.J. leaned across the bar and spoke softly, but firmly, to Angie.

She shrugged one shoulder and retreated a distance of two stools, where Hap, triggering a brief concert of metal on metal on denim on leather, surrendered his spot.

After a moment, with the usual greetings and the arrival of Carol's sauvignon blanc followed by Otis' pint, a reliable Madison IPA called Hopalicious, Angie took the floor.

"You can't tear that fuckin' place down," she growled.

"We're not—"

"Or even seal it off," Angie pressed. "It won't let you."

"It?" asked Crystal pointedly.

"Angie, come on. The building won't let us seal it off?" asked Carol. "What is it? Alive?"

Angie, whose stool now bordered Carol's, leaned close. "Lady, I don' know," she said. "But it definitely ain't dead."

"What? Haunted by the Kuckuck sisters?" said Maury sarcastically.

Crystal, tonight wearing a floor-length hibiscus-appliqué caftan with mother-of-pearl buttons and a scalloped white border, her hair wrapped in a matching scarf highlighted by a giant silk hibiscus blossom in vibrant crimson, said, "How do you know that, Angie? For that matter, how do you know anything about that old building?"

"What I know," said Angie, putting away half her margarita in a gulp, "is that John Stormwalker came away from there seriously shook up. I had to use up a whole bottle of good schnapps putting him to sleep. Until yesterday, I'd never seen anything faze that old rooster."

Carol burrowed straight to the point. "Stormwalker said, 'Remove the body.' What did he mean? What body?"

Angie dodged the question. "That building is under a spell ... or I don't know. And John couldn't say. There's a presence."

"What a load of crap," muttered Hap.

"C'mon, Angie. What do we got?" said Maury, who had set up on the far side of Otis. "Ho-Chunk vampires?"

"No!" Angie insisted, spilling tequila. "Whatever it is, it's not Ho-Chunk. It has nothing to do with any of our people. Or any other tribes. This is something else."

"Something else? What?" asked A.J. "From where?"

"I have no idea," said Angie. "Gimme another drink."

"Well then," A.J. replied, postponing Angie's margarita, "you really don't know what you're talkin' about, Angie. Where do you get off—"

Angie directed a cold stare that silenced A.J. She handed him her empty glass. "I get off because of John. You may think he's full of Indigenous shit—" She shifted her stare to Hap. "But he has found and walked the sacred path to the spirits of our ancestors."

"The Weyekins," said A.J.

"Yes, you remember. Good," said Angie. "John says he talks to them. I believe him."

"Yeah. Me, too," said Kenny.

"Kenny," said Crystal. "You wouldn't know a Ho-Chunk ancestor if she came up and bit you on the ass."

"Well, yeah," said Kenny, apologetically. "Most days, I can't even feel my ass."

"Can we, please?" said Carol.

Angie regained control. "Last week, after going into the building, John went home and entered a deep trance. I sat with him an hour, but he didn't even know I was there. When he finally came around, he said he had spoken with the Weyekins. He told them what he had seen in that place, and what he hadn't seen. He told the Weyekins how he felt."

"Okay, how did he feel?" asked A.J., handing Angie a fresh margarita.

"Frightened," said Angie. She took a sip. "John doesn't spend a lot of his life with a clear head. I think we all know that. He has potions and formulas and pipes full of stuff that, if it didn't kill most people, it would send us crawling the walls. John has had every nightmare and looked every monster in the eye. He doesn't scare."

"But this scared him?" said Carol.

"Yeah," said Angie. "Whatever it was in that building didn't want him there. He wasn't allowed. It wanted to kill him, but he couldn't understand why. He couldn't talk to it like he does with the Ho-Chunk spirits. He said the darkness was like the bottom of a grave. He couldn't see into it, couldn't hear anything or touch it. All he could do was feel, and all he could feel was anger ... hatred! He was trespassing in the house of death."

Otis caught Angie's eye. "I know the feeling."

"So, according to old John, there's a curse on the building," Maury said. "But it wasn't Stella who cast the spell. Right, Angie?"

Angie nodded, drank and looked tired.

"You know what we're getting around to here?" said A.J. "It's prejudice."

"Whatcha mean?" asked Hap.

"Okay, what happened? The last of the Kuckuck spinsters dies. The city ends up holding the bag and tryin' to collect rent from the last tenants up there," said A.J. "They don't pay because the town can't make 'em pay. So, to get 'em out of there, the town condemns the building—again—and they're evicted. The building goes empty and dark and spooky, and what happens? We start telling scary stories about the Indians who were the last to leave, Ronny Leaf, the troubled kid and his mother, this strange old full-blooded Ho-Chunk woman who sat by the window and gave folks the evil eye as they walked by."

Angie smiled at this.

"Yeah?" said Hap.

"But what about the other apartment?" said A.J. "Where the white people lived?"

"You mean, what's-his-name? Purlew?" said Maury.

"That's right," A.J. said. "Francis Purlew, known affectionately as 'Pyramid,' who was every bit—no, he was weirder than Stella Leaf. Most of what people said about her was what people made up about her. Pyramid Purlew was finger-in-the-socket weird in his own right."

"Remind me. Why did they call him 'Pyramid'?" asked Carol.

"I think it's because," began Crystal, "he had some sort of obsession with Egypt."

"Egypt?"

"Mummies," said Kenny in a tone of uncharacteristic clarity. "He talked about mummies all the time."

This was the longest sentence anyone had heard from Kenny in a month.

"Kenny, you talked to Purlew?" asked Crystal.

Kenny straightened up and took a firm grip on the bar. "Used to see 'im at the Roost, back before they took away my driver's license."

Kenny, who rarely drew this much attention, basked in its glow and cast A.J. a significant glance. A.J. moseyed down the bar, brought back a bottle of Grey Goose and filled Kenny's tumbler.

"He drank out there by himself," said Kenny, referring to the Red Rooster, the roadhouse east of Hercules on Highway 33. "Wouldn't stand anybody else one goddamn drink even if they saved his life from a pink elephant stampede."

Kenny savored this allusion as he sipped his vodka. "But then, he met this fella, out there, at the bar, at the Roost."

Kenny paused, weakened by the effort.

"What fella?" demanded Hap.

Crystal slugged Hap on the arm. "Quiet, you. Let Kenny talk."

"Thank ya," said Kenny. "Course, I didn't know who. Never seen him b'fore. But Stan, you know Stan, Chief?"

Otis said, "Yes, Kenny." He didn't bother to elaborate because Stan—Shea Stanke—had been proprietor and bartender at the Red Rooster since the Clinton administration.

"So, I says to Stan, whozat?" said Kenny. "Turns out it's this deer butcher over by La Valle, named Bewick."

"Bewick?" said Maury.

"Orlo," Kenny amended. "Orlo Bewick." Kenny finished his glass, and A.J. filled it.

"Like I said, Purlew didn't talk to nobody. But then, Stan tells 'im Orlo Bewick stuffs animals."

"Stuffs animals?" asked Hap.

"He's a taxidermist?" said Carol.

"No, no, no, no. He stuffs *animals*," said Kenny.

Carol nodded. "I stand corrected."

Kenny rolled on. "Yeah, well, so, anyway ..." Kenny took a vodka break, followed by a deep breath.

"Anyway, ol' Pyramid finds out ol' Orlo stuffs animals'n, all of a sudden, he's got a new buddy and he's buyin' drinks for the fella. And Orlo, he ain't lookin' no gift beer in the mouth. Thick as thieves, they was. Whew."

This last gasp ended Kenny's disquisition. He settled back around his tumbler of highfalutin vodka and dozed.

"Stuffed animals," said Crystal thoughtfully, "and mummies."

"Do you suppose," asked Maury, "this Orlo guy is still around?"

CHAPTER 19

(Wednesday, the 11th of June)

"Orlo Bewick?" said Maisie Hopkins as she poured Otis' coffee. "The deer butcher over in La Valle?"

"You know him?" asked Carol.

Maisie recoiled at the suggestion. "Orlo? Jesus God no. I only know *of* him. Even if I ever killed a deer, I wouldn't take it over to him. Word is he never cleaned his chainsaw—or any of his tools, or washed his hands, for that matter—since the day he went into business."

"When was that?" asked Carol.

"Right around 1990," said Minnie Trout, who suddenly emerged from behind Maisie.

"Minnie!"

"Maisie!"

The two women hugged chastely. Between them, no secret hidden in the boudoirs or buried beneath a thousand flat rocks in Hercules held any mystery. Minnie knew what was up before it happened, and Maisie had ferreted out every detail before breakfast wound down at Calamity Jane's.

"Shove over, Chief," said Minnie.

Overlooking the coincidence that Janis Joplin was singing "Move Over" on Calamity Jane's golden oldies soundtrack, Otis shifted toward the window and made room for Minnie.

Maisie scurried off and hurried back with coffee for Minnie. Then she anchored the edge of the booth, leaning toward Carol.

Minnie began as though she hadn't been interrupted. "Orlo's the salt of the earth, which means that nothing can grow wherever he goes and anything that was growing shrivels up and dies."

"That's quite vivid, Minnie," said Carol, "but I don't quite understand."

Maisie broke in. "You know that Sinatra song about New York, where it says, 'If you can make it here, you can make it anywhere'?"

"Yes," said Carol. "But I think Liza Minnelli sang it better."

Maisie let that pass, "Well, Orlo would be dead in a New York gutter in twelve hours. He can't make it anywhere."

"But isn't he making it ... where?"

"La Valle," said Otis, helpfully.

"Didn't Maisie just say he's in business there, butchering deer?" said Carol.

"Well, sweetheart, what you can't possibly know about Orlo is how he spent the forty-odd years before he got around taking up that just about worthless slaughterhouse," Minnie said.

"Well, no, I can't," said Carol. "I've never heard of this man."

"Nor has most anyone else," said Minnie. "Nor should they want to."

"Except," Maisie interjected, "for a few cheapskate deer hunters from Illinois, who wouldn't know a tenderloin from a tongue. There's a proper way of cutting up a deer, dear."

"And this Orlo doesn't know it," said Minnie.

"He's a butcher in the worst sense of the word," said Maisie.

"Excuse me," said Otis. "Minnie, you said Orlo Bewick had no, um ... job, for forty-some years?"

"Well if drinking was a job, yes," said Minnie. "If driving out onto the Interstate and picking up roadkill was a respectable job for a responsible adult, well yeah, I guess Orlo had a job."

"Roadkill?" said Carol, looking queasily at her breakfast. "He didn't ..."

"Eat it? No," said Minnie. "He tried to stuff it."

"He wanted to be a taxidermist," said Maisie. "But he never went to school and studied how to do it right."

"He could've got his head out of his behind and tried to learn from someone who knows what he's doing," added Minnie. "This is deer country, for God's sake. We got taxidermists behind every tree. Every bar in the state has deer heads on every damn wall, including the ladies rooms."

"No, not true," said Carol. "A.J. doesn't have any deer heads."

"That's right, hon," said Minnie. "And next time you see him, you should give him a great big thank-you kiss for being the only bartender in Wisconsin with any taste."

"I will."

"I'm losing track here," said Otis. "Orlo Bewick was jobless and uneducated. He was a drunk with no skills and no interest in anything except, apparently, the mangled corpses of animals. But he's in business—or he was. How'd that come about?"

Minnie nodded to Maisie, who explained. "Orlo's mother over in Lone Rock—that would've been Evelyn Bewick—she had an uncle who ran the Sinclair station in La Valle, until he died and the company couldn't find anyone to pick up the franchise for a gas station on Highway 33 with a daily revenue less than a hundred dollars. But it turned out that Evelyn's uncle owned the land and the station building, and she was next of kin. So she became a propertied woman but wasn't about to move to little La Valle from the big city of Lone Rock. So the uncle's filling station pretty much fell into ruin 'til Evelyn died, leaving the building and an acre of oil-soaked dirt to Orlo. But here's the proof that God looks over drunks and dimwits, 'cause Evelyn also left behind about a hundred thousand in savings. And you gotta hand it to Orlo. He could've drank up every undeserved penny left behind by his sainted mother. But he moved into that place, fixed the holes in the roof, passed himself off as a deer butcher and even put in a locker plant."

"Locker plant?" asked Carol.

"That's a big walk-in freezer, dear," said Minnie. "Used to be, every town in Wisconsin had a locker plant, 'cause not many people had freezers at home. You shoot a hundred-fifty-pound deer, you end up with sixty, eighty pounds of venison. You need a place to keep it."

"That's a locker plant?" said Carol.

"You got it," said Minnie.

"And Orlo has one."

"Last I heard. There's still a few around. Why, if I had a couple deers' worth of venison, I'd rather keep it somewhere other than my house."

"You wouldn't, Min," said Maisie. "You hate venison."

"It's like chewin' my shoes," said Minnie.

"You haven't tried Nita's venison stew," said Maisie, referring to Bonita McCullough, manager and chef of Calamity's.

"Well, if Nita cooked it," said Minnie, softening, "I might."

Otis intervened. "So, Orlo's given up roadkill?"

Minnie shook her head. "Last I heard, which was not recent, he was using the garage over there as his taxidermy studio."

A sudden clattering in the kitchen momentarily drowned out the voice of Connie Francis, yearning quadrophonically for "Where the Boys Are." The noise caught Maisie's attention. She looked at her watch.

"Oops," she said. "Break's over. Into the breach."

And she was gone.

"So, Orlo Bewick," said Otis, reviewing the case, "might still be alive and well, chopping up Bambi in La Valle. And I gather that he was Francis Purlew's only known friend. Is that right, Minnie?"

Minnie sipped and said, “If either of that unholy pair had any friends at all.”

“Yes, well, the evidence is thin,” said Otis. “Kenny Kelly, if you can believe him, said he saw them together at the Roost.”

“Excuse me,” said Carol. “But why do we care?”

Minnie answered this one. “Well, sweetie, it’s about the old Kuckuck building. There’s something about that place that’s scarin’ the bejesus out of our little kids. Everybody thought it was angry Indians put a jinx on the joint, but that don’t seem to be the problem. The only other suspect is Pyramid Purlew. He lived there.”

Carol considered this and said. “All right, so what do we know about Purlew, other than he was interested ... well, according to Kenny Kelly, in mummies? Minnie, what did he do for a living? Did he have a family? He was married, wasn’t he?”

Minnie’s eyes went all aglow. “Married? Well, now, there’s a story.”

“No, there isn’t. Not now,” said Otis. “We have to get to work. We’re late.”

CHAPTER 20

Anxious that the city council might send bulldozers up Main Street to flatten the Kuckuck building before he got a good look inside, Jim Otis moved fast to set up a proper search. As soon as he was in the office, he sicced Minnie on Hugo Harris, superintendent of the Department of Public Works.

She turned the call over to Otis. "Hugo, I need to turn the power back on at ... just a second. Minnie, what's the address there, upstairs?"

Minnie knew. Speaking on the extension, she said, "Hugo, it's 601½ East Main."

Harris said, "Can't do, Chief. By now, all the wiring is rat-chewed and rotten. We'd no sooner flip the switch that we'd have half the fire trucks in the county tryin' to keep that whole block from burnin' down."

Earl was also in the office. "It wouldn't be hard," he said, "to plug into the power on the streetlight there, and run a wire upstairs."

Otis relayed this idea to Harris. "Well, it'd take a hell of an extension cord," said Harris.

"Could you get one?" asked Otis.

"I guess."

"Need more'n one," said Earl.

"Can you get several, Hugo?" asked Otis.

"I guess," said Harris.

"By this afternoon?"

"Well, now ..."

"Chief, don't worry," said Earl. "I'll make sure we get plenty of extension cords. Lights, that's a little harder. But I'll talk to Lester Roh. He takes all the high-school yearbook pictures. He has all the lights we need."

"What about—"

"Don't worry, Chief. I'm on my way to the DPW garage right now. I'll rattle Hugo's cage."

"Thank you, Earl."

Just before three in the afternoon, Otis pulled his car up in front of the Kuckuck building, where Earl was presiding over a team of "professionals" that included photographer Lester Roh and the unexpected duo of Jerry Conklin and his son, Nelson. A curious crowd had gathered. Otis scanned the group for Riley Hawkins. He was relieved not to see him. It was, after all, a school day.

Otis took Earl out of anyone's earshot and nodded toward the Conklins, whose presence—in baggy jeans, work shoes, stained shirts and excessive hair, lent almost any scene an air of raffishness. "What are they doing here?" Otis asked.

Earl sighed. "Well, Hugo wasn't feelin' up to snuff," said Earl. "Said his hemorrhoids were acting up. He had two men filling potholes up where County UU comes into town and he couldn't pull 'em off the job. That's pretty much the whole DPW crew since Andy Hillerich retired and moved to Arizona with Sheila."

"So, the Conklins?"

"Well, you know Jerry," said Earl. "He'll take on just about any job. And the boy, Nelson, he's part of the package."

Otis shook his head. "Earl, that's thirty-eight dollars an hour—times two."

"Actually, Chief, it's forty-two. Jerry raised his rates."

Otis rolled his eyes and headed toward Jerry Conklin, who

styled himself as the town's all-purpose fix-it man, ready and able to cope with any technical or mechanical challenge. Jerry was leaning on a lamp post, a pile of heavy wires coiled near his feet.

"Chief."

"Hi, Jerry."

"Took the plate off the lamp post here, stripped the insulation, hooked in a few 'gator clips. You're ready to rock 'n' roll, Chief."

"I see," said Otis, looking at Jerry's son, who was smoking what appeared to be a controlled substance and kneading his crotch. "And what part of the job did Nelson handle?"

"Oh, the boy's a crack electrician, Chief. Couldn't've done this job without 'im."

Otis smiled. "I'm not sure Dani Whelihan's gonna buy that, Jerry," said Otis, referring to Hercules' town clerk. "She's known Nelson since grade school. I'd bear that in mind when you turn in your invoice."

He parted from Jerry Conklin without waiting for a reply.

Neither Conklin nor lighting supervisor Lester Roh volunteered to help Otis haul the extension cords up the staircase. Earl offered.

"No, I want you out here, Earl," said Otis, "in case something happens to me."

"Well, jeez, Chief, what could—"

"Just stay put, Earl, and watch my back."

"You got it, Chief."

Otis started toward the doorway, uncoiling a long extension cord as he progressed. In his other hand, he carried several shorter cords to be distributed among the rooms upstairs.

He was on the first step when he felt the old building strike back against him. The walls of the staircase closed in 'til they were barely wider than his shoulders. They writhed with coarse black bristles, their tips prodding him, stinging like horse nettle. The crawling, clinging tresses tangled his feet and brought him to his knees. He felt them slithering onto his back, pressing him down. Stubbornly, he struggled upright and climbed a step, another one. Leaning against the wall, he felt sudden pinches of pain on his arms and neck. He turned to look. From the strands of the Medusan wall, a sharp, narrow face with rows of fine teeth emerged and snapped at his cheek, ripping flesh away. Blood poured from the wound and ran down, dripping from his chin. He peered at his attacker, but it wasn't alone. The biting things covered the malevolent staircase, lunging toward him like bodiless coyotes, their jaws like scissors, nipping, tearing, pink tongues licking his blood.

Otis froze and closed his eyes. He shut out the steep black tunnel that clawed at him with its rage and refusal. Stubbornly, he remembered reality, seeing on his eyelids an empty staircase faintly visible in angled sunlight from a ravaged roof. He waited. He listened.

"Chief, you okay?"

Otis heard. He opened his eyes. He reached up and touched his face—gritty with dust captured in sweat. There was no blood. The steps were vague shadows before him, but there they were.

"I'm fine, Earl!"

Earl replied skeptically. "Okay, Chief. I was just—"

"I need you right there, Earl."

Once atop the stairs, Otis crept cautiously down a bleak hallway to the rear apartment, which would have been the last known dwelling of Francis Purlew and his wife, Elvira. The door opened noisily to a main room where shafts of weak light, through the seams in boarded windows, drew lines in a carpet of dirt. He dropped all the cords and headed back down.

"Whatever's got hold of this building," Otis said to Earl, "we haven't beat it. It's fighting back."

Otis grabbed one of Lester Roh's tripod-mounted studio lights and hurried back inside, expecting resistance. But the staircase relented. Inside the apartment, he set up the light, plugged it into the main extension cord and flipped a switch. Now, somehow, he felt as though he had forced a demon to retreat into its lair of shadows. He allowed himself a moment of relief.

Otis stepped into the hallway and shouted. "Earl, bring all the lights!"

After the cords had been stretched into all four rooms and the studio lights turned on, Otis surveyed an apartment as dreary as any he had ever entered in Chicago. Otis remembered what Bette Davis had said to Joseph Cotten in *Beyond the Forest*.

He stood in the middle of what was clearly a living room, with a floor that was once waxed hardwood, probably oak. Now, the wood was raw and sickly gray. Three doors were visible. To his left, a doorless bathroom contained a sink half-detached from the wall and a commode that looked as though it had been attacked with a sledgehammer. There was a shower stall, apparently made of tin, that had slipped its moorings to a point where it looked ready to topple onto a floor where half the black-and-white tiles were scattered helter-skelter on a layer of filth.

To Otis' right was a bedroom, which he had studied briefly while installing one of the lights. This connected to another bedroom. Both were bare, with the exception of the obligatory layer of dust. In a corner of the back bedroom, incongruously, Otis had found a squirrel dead so long that its remains were little more than a hollow-eyed pelt.

There was a kitchen that Otis could see on his left, at an angle. But the windows first caught his eye. In the living room, each pane was three feet tall, thirty inches wide. The back bedroom had an identical arrangement. In the summer, these vast single panes would have filled two rooms with light and oppressive heat. In the Wisconsin winter, with no insulation in the old building's brick and sheetrock walls, they would have turned the apartment into a meat locker.

"Jesus, Chief," said Earl. "The ceiling's what? Ten feet up? Ya couldn't heat this place."

"They tried," said Otis. Between the doorways to the bathroom and kitchen was a steel platform, its edges curled and dented. Around it, even through the dust, Otis could see a rim of dark stains, where heating oil had spilled and soaked into the floor.

"Jeez, Chief. They had one of those old oil stoves. It only got you warm if you stood like, two feet away."

As Otis looked around, John Stormwalker's benediction lingered in his mind:

"Remove the body."

There was no body. The apartment had been stripped naked.

In the two barren bedrooms, where the closets had been emptied and the doors torn away, there were no secret panels, no corpse-size window boxes, no cavities or protrusions. The bathroom was too small, too ruined, and probably too moldy to contain anything which, after a few years, would have rotted into a feculent residue.

But he was curious about the kitchen. He crossed the living room, pulling one of Lester's studio lights along. He aimed the light across the kitchen, then played his flashlight slowly around the room. To his left, the sink was a porcelain wreck, its bowl a Tchelitchew caricature of stains in black, brown and bilious green, its plumbing absent. A boarded-up window was broken and lightless. There were empty spaces and right-angled blemishes where a range and refrigerator once had resided. No furniture had survived the Purlew exodus, but remarkably, no one had bothered to rip from the wall a panel of cabinets. The doors were either gone or hanging by a hinge. Two feet of space above the cabinets was festooned with remnants of cobwebs long since forsaken, in the absence of edible insects, by the spiders who had spun them. Otis let his torchlight linger on the lacework of dusty webs, puzzled and pleased by the strange beauty that sometimes emerges from abandonment and decay.

"Hm," he said.

Earl, at Otis' elbow, said, "What?"

"Probably nothing," said Otis.

He moved the studio light, setting it precariously on the platform of the sink and aimed it at the ceiling above the cabinets.

"There's a seam," he said. "See it?"

"Sort of," said Earl, irresolutely.

"These buildings along Main," said Otis. "Did they have attics?"

"No idea. Prob'ly not."

"Well, what's that?"

"Search me, Chief."

"It looks to me like it might be the edge of a trapdoor. But it's hard to tell through all the dirt."

Earl was noncommittal.

"Earl?"

"Yeah?"

"We need a ladder."

True to his vocation, Jerry Conklin had a ladder in his truck. It took more than a half-hour for Earl and Jerry, with Nelson observing appreciatively, to wrestle the ungainly ladder up the narrow staircase and into the decrepit kitchen. With some concern for his still weak leg, Otis gingerly clattered upward. Reaching the cabinet top, he swept away the cobwebs. He stretched up, scraping at a layer of dust embedded in an accumulation of kitchen grease. Beneath, he found the contours of a panel whose wainscot surface differed from the smooth plaster of the ceiling.

"Looks like an attic," said Otis.

"No shit?" said Earl.

Nelson Conklin, the youngest and presumably most agile

of the crew, got the assignment of prying open the paint-sealed attic door and facing whatever grisly surprise might emerge from the black space beneath the ragged roof of the Kuckuck building.

After chipping away and spraying Otis, Earl and his father with a drizzle of dust and splinters, Nelson freed the panel from the ceiling. He passed it down. Earl set it aside.

"C'mon, Nellie. What's up there?" shouted Jerry Conklin.

"It's fuckin' dark. Somebody gimme a flashlight."

Otis' torch relayed up the ladder. Nelson braced himself on the opening and rose to the ladder's top step, causing it to wobble.

"Goddammit, hold it steady!"

Otis, Earl and Jerry gazed up as Nelson eased, shoulder deep, into the ceiling and pointed the flashlight into the darkness. A pregnant pause ensued.

Finally, "Jesus CHRIST!"

"What, what, what?" cried Earl.

"Jesus Christ!"

"Goddammit, Nelson! What?"

"Bottles!" shouted Nelson.

"What?"

Nelson crouched and turned, facing the others. "Bottles, goddammit."

"Bottles?" asked Earl. "Whaddya mean, like moonshine? What?"

"No, no," said Nelson. He plunged back into the attic, where his voice was muffled and sepulchral. "Huge bottles! With stuff in 'em!"

"What stuff?" demanded Nelson's father.

"Floating in 'em!" replied Nelson. "Floating stuff ..."

"In huge bottles," Otis concluded.

By six o'clock, after an ordeal of shifting, lifting and careful hefting, four jars of clear glass with wax-sealed lids had descended intact from what was probably Pyramid Purlew's secret storage space. They rested in a row on the back panel of Jerry Conklin's truck. The hinge-top jars, each with a capacity of at least three gallons, were liquid-filled with gray, squishy objects floating vaguely inside. The liquid was murky.

Otis, Earl, Jerry Conklin and his son, Nelson, were catching their breath. They were smeared with dirt, cobwebs in their hair, slightly abraded and mildly contused from their exertions. An ill-advised phone call, at mid-removal, had brought Minnie to the crowd. She had summoned Carol. Riley Hawkins, who had also sniffed out the expedition, stood at Otis' hip, staring at the four mysterious jars.

"What the hell," said someone in the crowd.

"Is this it?" asked Carol. "Is this the body?"

"What body?" replied Otis, testily. "This is just ... I don't know. I can't tell what's in the jars."

He might have continued complaining because he was tired, dirty and frustrated, but he was interrupted by his phone. His daughter was calling.

"Hi, Nat."

"Hiya, Daddy. What's happening? Didja find the monster in the building?"

"There's no monster in the—"

"Give me that?" Carol snatched the phone from Otis.

"Hello, Natalie," she said. "Your father's in no mood. He just got out of the building."

"Really? Wha'd he find?"

Carol patiently explained to Natalie what she knew about the ascent into Pyramid Purlew's attic, the removal of four strange bottles and the perplexity of her father over what seemed to be the pointless discovery of what were probably canned vegetables or preserved meat that had gone hideously rotten.

"Lemme see, lemme see," said Natalie, whose curiosity was fierce.

Dutifully, Carol trained Otis' phone on the row of jars, scanning them slowly. Natalie's voice interrupted the show.

"Oh!" she exclaimed excitedly. "I know what those are!"

"You do?" asked her father.

"Nah, she couldn't," muttered Jerry Conklin.

"She could," said Otis.

"What are they?" asked Carol.

"This is way cool," said Natalie.

"Natalie," Carol repeated, "what are they?"

"Yeah! C'mon!" shouted Riley.

Natalie's face, on the smartphone screen, was smug and all-knowing.

"They're canopic jars!"

A moment of collective incomprehension silenced the gathering.

"Okay, kid," said Otis at last, "what the hell is a colonic jar?"

"Canopic," Natalie replied, in a tone of triumphal erudition.

CHAPTER 21

Four huge jars stood in a row at A'Jay's. Before allowing them space on the bar, A.J. had dusted them, scrubbed the surfaces with Windex, sprayed them with Lysol and wiped them down with a clean bar cloth. Despite all these ablutions, the contents of the four containers were nebulous shapes floating in muddy fluid.

"So," said A.J., "what is this shit?"

Earl grunted dubiously. "And what are these symbols here s'posed to mean?"

He tapped a crudely drawn figure on one jar's exterior. It appeared to have been applied with Testors model paint, in bright red.

The voice of Natalie, piping up from Otis' phone, demanded to know what Earl was pointing to.

"There are symbols on the jars," said Carol.

"Symbols? Great!" Her voice shrill with excitement, Natalie demanded, "Tell me, tell me, tell me! Does one of them look like a dog?"

Earl peered at the markings on all four jars and said, "Jesus, it does—sort of. How'd the kid know that?"

"Show me!" shouted Natalie.

Carol aimed the phone's viewfinder at the doglike figure on the jar.

"This is so cool!" exclaimed Natalie. "That's gotta be Duamutef!"

"Du who?" asked Earl.

"Duamutef! He's one of the sons of Horus. There are four of them." Natalie rattled off four names, including Duamutef. "They travel with the dead person through the underworld to the Field of Reeds. They help protect the soul from being eaten by Ammut."

"Excuse me," said Crystal, who was voluminous this evening in silk harem pants and a shirt that looked as though Errol Flynn had worn it in a pirate movie, "but what the hell is the girl talking about?"

"Hi, Crys!" shouted Natalie.

"Hello, sweetie."

"How'd you know that?" Earl repeated.

Natalie explained, "Oh, y'see, for my project in World History, I'm doing Egypt. I've been reading up on ancient Egypt—mummies and tombs and Thebes and pyramids and stuff—for *months.* I really love it, but nobody wants to talk about it. Well, except Ms. Hopwood. She's my teacher, and she says I'm absolutely gonna get an A. But wow, I mean, you found *canopic jars* in Hercules? Wow! I gotta see 'em!"

"You're seeing them right now, kid," said Otis.

"No, no! I mean in person! Canopic jars! Awesome!"

"Well," said Otis, "you'll be coming up—"

"Daddy! You know what's in 'em?"

"Well, it's hard to tell."

"I can!"

"You can?" asked Crystal.

"Yeah! It's organs! From a *mummy*! No, wait, not from the mummy. The Egyptians took 'em out before they mummified the, um … dead person."

"Wait a minute, Nat," said Carol. "You're saying that these jars have human body parts inside?"

"Well, yeah! Stomach, liver, lungs and intestines. But not the heart. They leave the heart inside the body. But d'ya know what they did with the *brain*?"

"I don't think I want to know," said Carol.

"Oh no! You wouldn't!" said Natalie. "It's totally gross. The Egyptians had no respect for brains at all!"

"Natalie, I promise you. These are not human organs," said Otis deflatingly.

"Really?" asked Natalie, suddenly disappointed.

"How do you know that, Jim?" asked Crystal.

"Well, it's a simple matter—"

"I don' know, Chief. I can't tell what's in there," said Hap, elbowing past Earl and almost touching a jar with his nose. "A.J., can you?"

"Not really."

"Y'know, it could be human organs," said Hap. "Could be anything."

"It could be nothing," snapped Otis.

A half-dozen bar patrons had left stool and booth to crane over the shoulders of Otis and Carol, Earl and Crystal, Kenny, Hap and the judiciously silent Teddy, at the four canopic containers.

"Shouldn't we open one up?" said someone in the crowd.

"No," said Otis. "Not 'til we know more about them."

"They could explode," suggested Earl.

"They could be evidence," said Crystal.

"Of what?" asked Earl.

"We are not opening those things," declared A.J. "Not on my premises."

"I've seen jars like that," said Hap, "when I was in school and we had this class trip to the Field Museum. They had creatures in jars, snakes and lizards and pig fetuses, stuff like that."

"Preserved in formaldehyde," added Carol helpfully.

"Yeah," said Hap. "But at the museum, you could see what they were. These jars here. It's too cloudy to tell."

"Well then, Jimmy, you don't actually know for sure," Crystal persisted. "Those things in the jars just might be human organs—like your daughter says."

"No, it can't," said Otis.

"I hate to say, but Daddy might be right," offered Natalie from Otis' phone on the bar.

This quieted the discussion.

Natalie elaborated. "Y'see, according to Egyptian burial rituals, which I've read about, the jars go into the tomb after the mummy is all dried out and wrapped up. Sometimes, the Egyptian priests took the organs out of the jars and packed them back inside the mummy. Either way, the organs and the mummy got buried together. That was the rule."

"Okay," said Earl.

"So," said Natalie, "whe-ere's the mummy?"

Another silence.

"Daddy, you gotta keep looking."

"Sorry, kid, we searched everywhere. No mummy," said Otis, attempting a note of finality.

"No, wait," said Natalie. "Hey, Earl!"

"Yeah?"

"One of the jars has a dog's head on it, right?"

Earl hedged. "Well, it sort of looked like a dog."

"Okay, if there's a dog on one jar," Natalie said pedantically, "there has to be a jar with a man's face on it. Is there?"

"Yes, there is!" said Crystal emphatically.

"That would be the liver jar," said Natalie, "protected by the god Imseti."

"Okay, what about the other two?" offered Hap. "One of 'em looks sorta like a bird."

"A hawk?" asked Natalie, her excitement audible again.

"Yeah, it's a hawk," said Hap.

"All right!" said Natalie. "So, the other one, it's a baboon, right?"

"I was wondering what that was," said Earl.

"You're right, sweetie," Crystal said. "A really ugly baboon."

"Okay, y'see?" said Natalie. "Those are the symbols of the four sons of Horus, whose job is to protect the human organs inside the jars, which means, Daddy, there's gotta be a mummy."

"There's no mummy, kid," Otis reiterated. "And the stuff in the jars, well, we can't tell. It could be a cat that died, or a big fish or the biggest zucchini of the summer. People preserve things that other people would just throw away or bury."

"You mean," said A.J. suggestively, "like organs from bodies they stole from a graveyard?"

"No, Aje, don't go there," said Otis.

"I think he just went there," said Crystal.

"Oh, Jesus," said Hap, "you mean like Ed Gein, who dug up all those bodies up north?"

"Yes!" said Crystal. "And ate their liver with fava beans and a nice Chianti?"

"Goddammit, just a minute!" said Otis, losing his patience.

"Y'know, it wouldn't hurt," said A.J. soothingly, "to have the contents of these mystery jars analyzed, someplace other than my place of business, like, for instance, up at the state crime lab."

Otis shook his head. "Crime lab?" he said. "There's no crime here. Just stuff we found in the attic of a building that's been empty for God knows how long."

"But what would the harm—"

"Harm?" snapped Otis. "That lab is hip-deep in evidence of actual crimes. I can't even picture the reception I'd get if I walked in there with four jars full of slime soaked in alcohol. Podunk cops like me get no respect at all from those guys. I'd be a laughingstock for the rest of my alleged career."

This quieted the group. The rubberneckers began to return to stools and booths.

"Daddy's right," said Natalie at last. "Even if those are canopic jars and even if there really are livers and lungs and stuff in there, we're missing the most important thing."

"The mummy," said Crystal.

"There is no mummy," said Otis wearily.

"We should look for the mummy," said Hap. "I'll help."

"Oh," moaned Kenny, "miss my mummy."

"By all means, go off on a wild mummy chase. In the meantime," said A.J., "I'll keep the jars here, under the bar. Sealed tight, safe and sound."

"Or I could just drive them over to the landfill," said Otis, mostly to himself. "Or drop them in the quarry."

"You know what I think? I think he must've taken it away," said Crystal.

"Taken what away?" asked Earl.

"Who took it away?" asked Hap.

"Pyramid Purlew, of course," said Crystal. "He removed the mummy."

"No," said Otis.

"Where?" asked Hap.

"We have to look for it," said Crystal, pressing the issue.

A.J. complicated matters. "If we don't find the mummy, we'll never be able to remove the curse."

"Curse?" said Natalie.

"Yeah, kid," said A.J. "There's a curse on the Kuckuck building. It tried to kill your dad."

"Really?"

"No," said Otis. Carol patted his hand.

"Think about it. Purlew was into everything Egyptian, right? Like Nat," said A.J. "Those were *his jars*. He had to protect 'em, right? So, he calls down the wrath of all the gods of Egypt, to the Kuckuck building. And they put up this giant invisible No Trespassing wall! They curse the building."

"Whoa, really?" said Natalie. "Cool."

"I love it," said Crystal.

"No," said Otis.

Crystal ignored Otis. "So, let's say this Purlew person really put human organs in the jars. Where'd he get 'em? Was he out there exhuming bodies from cemeteries?"

"He must've been," said Hap. "I mean, look at Ed Gein. It's like a Wisconsin tradition!"

"Yes, like cheese," said Crystal, smiling crookedly, "and the Packers."

A.J. resumed the floor. "Anyway, what we know for sure is that the last of the Kuckuck sisters died and Pyramid Purlew had to clear out of the building. But let's just say he's got a half-mummied dead body up there that he dug up from Oak Grove Cemetery, and he can't exactly leave it behind, 'cause sooner or later, somebody's gonna find it. So, he hauls it away and buries it somewhere. Who knows where? But, he keeps the organs in the jars and leaves 'em behind, in the attic. Who knows why?"

"Right," said Otis. "Why ruin a good story with a motive?"

"Quiet, you," said Crystal.

A.J. was still thinking. "Okay, here's why Purlew left the jars behind. The Leaf family was still living down the hall. The S&Q was still selling hardware. Purlew couldn't take the chance to go back inside and get the jars 'til the building was empty. So, in the meantime, he calls on the gods of Egypt. Nat, which ones?"

"Osiris, Isis, Anubis."

"Good. Purlew calls down those gods. And they put a curse on the Kuckuck building. Anyone who sets foot past the doorway, they get scared shitless. You were scared shitless, right, James?"

Otis scowled.

"Oh yeah," said Earl. "He was!"

"But then, Purlew never got the jars," said A.J. "He died

before he could go back upstairs."

"A.J., that's great. But where did he take the mummy?" asked Natalie.

"There was no mummy," said Otis.

"Maybe it wasn't a mummy," said Crystal. "It might've been just a dead body. I mean, making mummies isn't easy, right, kid?"

"No," said Natalie, "you need a lot of tools. And chemicals, like natron and palm wine, embalming fluid ..."

"It occurs to me," offered Otis, "that the organs in these annoying jars might be from deer. The mummy we're all talking about was probably a dead doe picked up off the shoulder of I-90."

Otis looked at Kenny. "We have it on Kenny's unimpeachable authority that Purlew's only friend on earth was a deer butcher with a fetish for roadkill—Orlo ... Kenny, what was his name?"

"Er." Kenny stirred from a light doze. "B'wick," he murmured. "Yer assolutely right, Chief."

"This Orlo. Is he still in business?" asked Hap.

"My guess, he's dead," said A.J.

"You should check that out, Chief," said Earl.

"Yes, you should, Earl."

"I can," said Teddy, breaking his discreet silence.

"On your own time," said Otis.

"I wonder. Can you mummify a deer?" asked Crystal.

Natalie had the answer. "You can mummify anything."

"Good. Let's mummify this conversation," said Otis, with an air of menace. "A.J., my glass is empty."

CHAPTER 22

(Saturday, the 14th of June)

By consigning the four mysterious jars to a space beside A'Jay's beer cooler, Otis had—he thought—tabled the issue of Pyramid Purlew's curse. Having surrendered its secret, the Kuckuck building posed no further interest, even to Riley Hawkins. The city council could either tear it down or leave it be.

Otis directed his interest to Moving Day. Carol had charmed Dale Gundlach into terminating her lease as of June 15. Natalie bused up from Chicago on Friday the 13th to help with the move. Otis and Natalie, a crew of Carol's fellow teachers, A.J. and his family and Otis' growing circle of Hercules friends helped transfer all the boxes and useful furniture to Otis' cabin on Lake Hercules. The move was finished by six o'clock, in time for Otis to grill three steaks on the back patio. Otis, Carol and Natalie dined indoors, lest the mosquitoes drain their blood and leave them shriveled, mummy-like, in the weeds behind the cabin.

Over peach cobbler with ice cream, Carol made teacherly overtures to Natalie about the funerary rituals of ancient Egypt.

Natalie went gushy. "The cool thing," she said, "was the Egyptians thought dying was like good and bad, night and day.

Y'see, the thing is, when you die, you're not, like, gone. You're switching over, from life to afterlife—which the Egyptians thought was a better life, 'cause death goes on forever. I mean, they figured that things had to be better after you died, 'cause Egyptians didn't live that long. Tutankhamun was only about twenty-two when he died."

"Really?" said Carol encouragingly. "I had no idea."

"Yeah, but getting into the afterlife wasn't easy," Natalie continued, "'cause, even before you were allowed to become a mummy—I mean, you had to have a body to take with you into the afterlife, that's why they had mummies—you had to prove that you were a good person when you were alive."

"And how would I prove that I was good?" asked Otis.

"Well, Daddy, I'm sorry. You prob'ly couldn't."

"Thanks, kid."

"But I could," said Carol.

"Oh yeah! Of course," said Natalie.

She took a deep breath. She was boiling over with the knowledge she had accumulated in two months of commuting, over her mother's objections, through the dangerous city to the University of Chicago Library and its Egyptian collection.

"Look, y'have to understand that the Egyptians didn't think the earth was round. They thought the sun went underground every night and the sun god—his name was Ra—would take this boat trip every night through the underworld—and come back up in the morning. Well, when you died in Egypt, the dead person—who wasn't really dead—would have to take the same—"

"Wait. Explain," said Carol pedagogically. "How can a dead person not be dead?"

"Well, even in Egypt in the good old days, a lot of dead people stayed dead," said Natalie eagerly. "That was the whole point of mummies. You had to save the person's body because he, or she, they were gonna go on living in their afterlife. But you couldn't do it if your body was all rotted or burnt or you got killed someplace outside of Egypt. Egyptians had to die *in Egypt*, y'see. Or they were just, like, wasted."

"Okay, kid," said Otis. "So, if you wanted to live after you were dead, you had to go through the underworld?"

"Yeah, you got it, Daddy. But it wasn't easy. It was like getting your dream job—like police chief in Hercules—or getting into Harvard or something."

"Explain," said Carol, enjoying herself.

"Okay, so, if you were good ... I mean, if you'd lived a good life, getting through the underworld was like you're going to Heaven, only before you get there, you had to get past Saint Peter at the gate. Only in Egypt, there were, like forty-two Saint Peters, okay?"

"Okay," said Carol encouragingly.

"Right. So, you were down there and you met Osiris, who was like the god of the underworld and he's really important 'cause he had the power of *akh*, which if you don't have it, you can't rise from the dead."

"Ock?" said Otis.

"And you get your *akh* from Osiris?" asked Carol.

"Or from other gods, like Isis and Horus, but if you're working your way to the afterlife, Osiris was your best bet," said Natalie. "Anyway, if you didn't deserve to get *akh*, which meant you lived a bad life, then you just end up dead. Totally, okay?"

"You gotta have *akh*," said Otis.

"Right, Daddy, so you take this trip, on the boat that Ra rides every night through the underworld. Y'know, when I think about this, it's like that movie with the Rock, who's guiding this tourist boat through the jungle and the Rock is Ra—"

"Rock?" asked Otis. "Is that like *akh*?"

"Oh my God, Daddy."

"Dwayne Johnson is called the Rock," said Carol. "He's an actor, has a lot of muscles."

"He used to be a wrestler," added Natalie.

“The movie was called *Jungle Cruise*, right?” said Carol.

“Yeah,” said Natalie. “It was fun. You should see it, Daddy.”

“I’ll make a point of it,” said Otis. “But what does this Rock have to do with *akh*?”

“’Cause the underworld is like the Rock’s jungle cruise, okay? There are twelve regions you have to pass through (’cause that’s how many hours there are every night. Cool, huh?). And as you go through, there’s burning lakes and snakes and monsters and if you don’t know their names, they’ll climb up into the boat and attack you and you might not make it to the afterlife. But if you’ve got *maat*, which means you were a good do-bee while you were alive, you have lots of help. Anubis, whose sort of like the captain of the boat, guides you through, but you also have help from these four other sort of gods, the sons of Horus, whose names—”

“You’ve already told us, kid. Just go on.”

“Okay, right, so you’ve got this team, Osiris and Anubis and the four sons of Horus plus these four goddesses, all showing you the way,” said Natalie. “But, before you can head for the Field of Reeds, which is like Heaven, you have these forty-two other gods who judge whether you’ve committed any of the forty-two sins that could ruin your whole death.”

“Forty-two sins?”

“Yeah, sins—like killing someone, or stealing or like killing and cheating people out of money, or badmouthing one of the gods, or making someone cry or taking milk away from children—stuff like that,” said Natalie. “And you can’t get even one answer wrong. If you do, tough noogies. But even if you pass all forty-two tests, you’re not done ’cause you still gotta be weighed.”

“Weighed?” asked Carol. “Being fat is a sin?”

“No, no, no,” said Natalie. “There’s this balance thing.”

“A scale?”

“Right, yeah, a scale,” said Natalie. “It’s got these two bowls on either side, right? Anubis takes the dead person’s heart and he puts it in one of the bowls. That's 'cause the heart holds the whole record of the person's life. And on the other side, Anubis puts in the dead person's *maat*, which looks like an ostrich feather. It's a symbol of whether the dead person was good or bad. If the two sides balance, then the dead person passes. But if the heart is heavier than the feather, then Ammut gets to eat the heart."

"Ammut?"

"Yeah, Ammut is like the devil, I think. He has the head of a crocodile. Half his body is a lion and the other half is a hippo."

"And if Ammut eats your heart?" asked Carol.

"It's all over," said Natalie. "No afterlife. You're dead."

Carol began to clear the dessert dishes.

"So," said Otis. "To get into this Field of Weeds."

"Reeds, Daddy."

"Right. To get there and live in the afterlife, you had to preserve your body. You had to be made into a mummy."

"But that wasn't easy," said Natalie. "I read all about it."

"I can tell," said Otis.

"Yeah, and the first thing you had to do, to make a mummy," Natalie rambled on, "you had to take out all the guts—except the heart—and save 'em, so you could dry out the whole inside of the body so it wouldn't start to go all rotten and putrid, y'see?"

"I see," said Otis. "And I'm guessing that the mortician put the guts into jars, in some sort of embalming fluid."

"Yeah!" Natalie enthused. "Canopic jars. Just like the ones you found. Y'see, that's the whole point, Daddy. If there's jars full of guts, there's gotta be a mummy."

"If you're right, Nat," said Carol, "if there is a mummy ..."

"Yeah?"

"Who's the mummy? Who died? And where is he?"

"Or she?" added Natalie.

While they washed the dishes, Otis kept up the interrogation. Under the assumption that he was asking a pertinent question, he said, "Were you inspired to research mummies because of the movie?"

"Movie? You mean *The Mummy*?"

"Yes."

"Oh, Daddy, gag me with a shovel!" exclaimed Natalie. "That movie was terrible. They got everything all wrong."

"Oh," said Otis. "They did?"

"Totally!"

"Everything?"

"Daddy, they screwed up right from the beginning. The movie starts at Hamunaptra, which they called the city of the dead. But there's no Hamunaptra, Daddy! There never was. They just made it up!"

"Well," offered Otis cautiously, "isn't that what movies are supposed to—"

"And y'know what really pissed me off? They made Anubis into a monster," said Natalie, almost shouting. "That wasn't fair. Anubis helps people through the underworld and protects them from being attacked by Ammut."

"Ammut, the crocodile god?"

"Right, yes, sort of."

"So, the movie slandered Anubis," said Carol.

"Yeah, but that wasn't the worst thing they did in that stupid movie."

Otis and Carol knew better than to speak, knowing that Natalie was bursting with data.

"You know the part where they went into the tomb at Hamunaptra—*which never existed!*—and they found a bunch of canopic jars?"

"Um, vaguely."

"I remember," said Carol.

"Okay, so," said Natalie, "how many were there?"

Otis was stumped. Carol took a guess. "Four?"

"No!" shouted Natalie. "There should've been four. But there were five! The Egyptians *never* had five jars. There were only four. But that's not the worst thing."

"Okay," Otis said, "what's the wrong thing?"

"D'ya know what they said was inside the stupid extra jar?"

Otis looked to Carol. Carol shrugged.

Natalie trumpeted, "The heart!"

"This I remember," said Otis. "The Egyptians would have left the heart inside the mummy, right?"

"That's right," said Natalie. "Because the heart was the mummy's brain and his soul. It's where his *maat* was. If you took out the heart, the dead person would be really, really dead."

"Oh, ya gotta have heart," crooned Otis softly, "miles and miles—"

"Hush," said Carol.

"And whose heart was s'posed to be in the extra jar, huh?" asked Natalie, rhetorically. Tell me that."

"I've got no idea," said Otis.

"Okay, Daddy, who was the mummy in *The Mummy*?"

"Who? You mean ... his name."

Natalie sighed impatiently, "It was Imhotep, okay?"

"I'll take your word for it, kid."

"Imhotep was the priest who fell in love with Anck-sunamun, the pharaoh's wife."

Otis nodded but kept his lip buttoned.

Natalie continued. "Well, there's the thing, Daddy. They couldn't've put Imhotep's heart in the stupid jar—or any of his parts. Y'know why?"

"This I remember," said Carol. "He was buried alive."

"Yeah! Right! They didn't cut anything out of him, except his tongue."

If Otis and Carol thought Natalie was finished, they were wrong.

"And did you see the jars?" Natalie raved on. "In the movie?"

"I guess," said Otis, straining his memory.

"So, what was wrong with them?"

Otis shrugged. "You tell me, kid."

"They were too small!"

"Too small?"

"They were like those cute coffee mugs you buy in the gift shop, Daddy," said Natalie. "D'ya think you could fit somebody's lungs, or their intestines, into a coffee mug?"

"I don't think I'd want to try, Nat."

"So, you're saying," Carol said, "the movie is ill-conceived."

"Totally!"

"Still," said Carol, "I thought it was kind of fun."

"Yeah, well, I thought so, too," said Natalie, "until I knew the truth. But I still like Rick."

"You mean Brendan Fraser?" said Carol.

"Yeah, he's cute."

"Hm, well, I suppose," said Carol pensively. "But I prefer a more sensitive, poetic sort of man."

"I sure hope you can find one someday," replied Natalie.

They exchanged mischievous smiles.

CHAPTER 23

(Monday, the 16th of June)

Because Natalie was out of school for the summer, Otis kept her 'til Monday and put her on a late morning bus to Chicago. Natalie hadn't ceased to spill funerary esoterica about ancient Egypt until Sunday evening, when she finally changed the subject to her friend Debbie Albright's flirtation with a tenth-grade boy and—more salient to Otis—her mother's date with a divorced Aetna Insurance executive named Marlon something.

"What do you know about this Marlon?" asked Otis.

"Nothin'," said Natalie. "You know how sneaky Mom is. She's like a sphinx."

Connie, Otis' ex, had had a traumatic "affair" with one of her continuing education professors, Paul Fazio, who proved to be more interested in Natalie than Connie. Hence, Otis was vigilant about his former wife's love life.

"Well, dig into it, kid. I want dirt on Marlon."

"I will, Chief. But Mom's like—"

"A sphinx."

Otis could squeeze no more Marlon data before Natalie boarded the bus.

"I expect a report."

"I'll think about it, Daddy."

They hugged, the bus door closed and Natalie was Illinois-bound.

Just shy of noon, Otis arrived at the police station. He thanked Earl for standing an extra shift and began to equip himself for an hour's patrol around Hercules.

"Not yet, Chief," said Minnie from her dispatcher's platform.

"I'm late as it is."

"Nobody's on the edge of their seat watching for you to drive by," said Minnie. "Besides, I've got something here."

"Something?"

"All that talk about mummies last week, and then the ghost of Ed Gein, kind of tickled my memory," said Minnie, a woman of formidable mnemonic powers.

"Yes?" Otis prompted.

"I remembered some entries in the police log from when Nate was chief."

Nate Neitzel, Otis' forebear, had been chief of police long enough to qualify as a local institution. He wielded so much political influence that he convinced the town council to pass an ordinance making the head of the Hercules Police Department an elective office with a four-year term. This made Nate the only elected police chief in the state, shielding him from the meddlesomeness of local politicians. This anomaly should have shielded Otis, too. But when accusations spread through town that Otis had made untoward advances toward Josie Dobbs, the council saw fit to override the "Neitzel Rule" and fire Otis after less than a year in office. They justified this exception by noting that Otis had been appointed, not elected, after Nate's sudden death.

Otis addressed Minnie. "So, you've been reading up on Hercules' criminal history?"

"That's right."

"And you found what?"

"Well," said Minnie, bouncing from her chair and plopping a stack of ledger-style books on Otis' desk. "I found a crime wave."

"Crime wave?"

"Dogs and cats disappearing all over town," said Minnie. "And look here!"

The old police logs were written in a crabbed and idiosyncratic shorthand unique to its author, who was now dead and unavailable as interpreter.

"I can't read that," said Otis.

"I can," crowed Minnie. "I had to send reports to the sheriff's office."

"So, what does it say?"

"Well, here," said Minnie, pointing at a line of Neitzel's glyphs. "Nate made notes about how the same thing was happening outside of town, on farms. There were pigs gone missing. And one of George Rostopov's goats."

"When was this?" asked Otis.

"Two thousand and five, and the next year, too."

"I see. And these animals weren't just wandering off?"

Minnie delivered one of her withering scowls. "No, Jimmy. Pets and pigs don't abscond in groups. Somebody was stealing Fido and Fluffy and Porky."

"Well, that's interesting, Minnie, but—"

"Yeah, well, what's more interesting is that Nate had his eye on none other than Francis Purlew as the dog, cat and pig purloiner."

"Purloiner?"

"Thief, Chief."

"I know." Otis returned Minnie's scowl. "He suspected Purlew?"

"Yes, sir."

"But he found no evidence?"

"No, but he dropped in on him one day." She flipped several pages in the log. "That's right ... let's see ... yes, in August of '06."

"Dropped in?"

"Yes. Upstairs at the Kuckuck building. That's where Purlew and Elvira were still living."

"And there was no evidence that our friend, Pyramid Purlew, was turning kidnapped kittens into little furry mummies?"

"Well, Nate found books."

"Books?"

"Yes, on ancient Egypt. Purlew had a whole bunch of them."

"Wasn't that Purlew's hobby?"

"Yes, it was. That's why Nate was suspicious about the man. But he didn't find anything but the books. And then ..."

"Then?"

"Well, September of '06, just like that. No more disappearing pets."

"And there were no grave robberies? No shades of Ed Gein?"

"Don't be silly, Jim," said Minnie authoritatively. "Ed Gein's bodies were all embalmed before he dug 'em up. If Purlew was making mummies, he needed fresh corpses, straight out of their deathbed, untouched by the undertaker."

"So, Minnie, you're leading me to a dead end here?"

"No, Jimmy. I'm leading you to how Pyramid Purlew obviously had a hidey-hole for all of his dogs and cats and piggies. But, after Big Nate started poking around, he couldn't risk any more petnapping. So, he changed his M.O."

"M.O.?"

"Yes, Jimmy. He found another source for the bodies he needed. Like maybe a guy who stuffs the animals he finds dead by the side of the Interstate ... Jimmy."

"You're suggesting, Minnie," said Otis deliberately, "that Pyramid Purlew teamed up with ... um, name?"

"Orlo Bewick," said Minnie, "the I-90 roadkill ghoul."

"Y'know, Minnie," said Otis, "this is the sort of cock-and-bull story that gets conspiracy theories started."

Minnie protested, but Otis was late to his noon patrol.

"I'll think about it," he said consolingly as he left the office.

But he didn't.

CHAPTER 24

(Tuesday, the 17th of June)

Although his efforts were sincere, Otis could not escape the speculation that had infiltrated the village of Hercules over the weird goings-on upstairs of the S&Q Hardware. During his patrols, he couldn't help noticing little popinjay clusters near the Kuckuck building's doorway, which he had ordered Jerry Conklin to board up. The plywood slabs nailed across the entrance had only served to elevate curiosity.

Someone, very likely Riley Hawkins, had spray-painted a warning that read: BEWAIRE THE CURSE!!!

Otis had refused all conversation on the overblown mystery, even with Carol, but it descended on him when he was trapped in his window booth at Calamity Jane's. Maisie was pouring coffee and Bobby Vinton was crooning "Blue Velvet" throughout the diner.

"They were a strange couple," said Maisie in a provocative undertone.

Otis didn't take the bait. He had cleared the Kuckuck building and had spent the weekend listening to his daughter's tutorial on Egyptian funereal rituals. As far as he was concerned, the case was closed. More important matters were preying on his psyche.

Carol, however, was still curious. "Who were the strange couple?" she said.

Otis sighed in defeat. Maisie's eyes lit up. "Oh, well, Elvira and Frank, the Purlews."

Carol was eager. "Really? How were they strange?"

Otis broke in, using his police-detective interrogation voice. "Maisie, how can you say that? Did you know them?"

"Well, not personally ..."

"For a while, they came in here," said Nita McCullough, the head wrangler of Calamity's, as she arrived with Otis' and Carol's breakfast plates. "They were one of those couples who sat across from each other and barely spoke."

"They weren't exactly lovey-dovey," added Maisie.

"So," said Otis, "they were a typical old married couple who had nothing to say to each other. This hardly qualifies as strange."

"Well, yes," said Maisie, "except that they didn't hardly talk to anybody else, either. They had no friends at all. And Elvira had this habit of comin' and goin'."

"Coming and going?" asked Carol, perking to this new information. "Going where?"

"She had family over in Minnesota, from what I heard," said Maisie.

Nita, who had stationed herself beside Maisie, pitched in. "Mankato."

"Yeah, Mankato," said Maisie.

Bobby Vinton faded out, giving way to Dusty Springfield "Wishin' and Hopin'."

"Elvira would just up and slip quietly out of town, and she wouldn't come back 'til—"

"Just a second," said Otis. "If Elvira had no friends, how did anybody know she was gone?"

Maisie rolled her eyes at Otis' urban ignorance. "Well, 'cause suddenly old Pyramid—Frank—he was suddenly doin' all the grocery shopping. At Burnstad's."

"Oh."

"Elvira always shopped at Shutter's."

"Oh."

"Besides, she always took the bus when she took off to Mankato," Maisie said pointedly. "Always bought her ticket from Lester Munk, who's never shy about tellin' anyone and his uncle about who's blowin' town."

"Okay, so there was a witness to when she split," said Otis. "But she didn't have to go through Lester when she returned. Or if she returned."

"Right you are, Chief," said Maisie. "Lester couldn't exactly see outside his ticket cage when folks unloaded off a bus. So, he couldn't say exactly when Elvira came back. But she always did, eventually."

"And how do we know that?" Otis pressed.

"Well, 'cause of Andy Sturtevant's bellyaching."

"Sturtevant?"

"Remember?" said Carol. "He ran that hardware store, downstairs."

"How could I forget?" said Otis. "So, what was his complaint?"

"Well, then," said Maisie, warming to the tale. "Elvira always traveled with this big old metal suitcase, which was too heavy for her. I don't guess she weighed over a hundred pounds, soakin' wet. So, that suitcase. She didn't so much carry it as just drag it along. So, when she got home, Andy knew she'd arrived, 'cause she'd be bumpin' that suitcase up a step at a time, banging into the wall of the hardware and knocking stuff off his shelves. Once, she tipped over a whole display of Coleman lamps, made a hell of a ruckus, busted glass all over the place. Andy pitched a fit, ran out of the store and yelled up the stairs at Elvira. And she didn't even turn around to see who was yellin' at her or why. Just kept bangin' up the steps, one at a time."

"So," said Carol, "the grapevine kept tabs on Elvira."

"Of course," said Maisie. "People talked for weeks about that tiff."

"But, in the end," Nita added with a note of intrigue, "no one was keeping tabs on the Purlews. It wasn't until after Andy Sturtevant closed down his store and headed south that people noticed that both Purlews were gone."

"Together?" asked Carol.

"Y'know," said Maisie, thoughtfully, "by the time that back apartment upstairs in the Kuckuck building emptied—nobody living there—I don't guess anybody'd seen Elvira for quite a while."

"How long?" asked Carol. "A year?"

"Maybe longer," said Maisie. "But heck, Carol. It wasn't like anybody ever looked for the woman, or expected to see her."

"I see," said Carol. "So, nobody knows whatever became of Elvira?"

"Like Maisie says, it's not as if anybody cared," Nita said. "Nobody knew the woman. Nobody ever missed her. Nor her husband, either."

"So," said Crystal that night at A'Jay's, "Elvira could've died up there."

Maisie was not available to advance Crystal's proposition. But Maisie was hardly necessary. Everyone in a bar is a theorist, and the theories had found focus on the wraithlike Elvira. "There were people who wondered about that," said A.J. as he set down Carol's wine glass.

He went on. "I mean, in a town like this, when someone isn't seen for a month at a stretch, there's someone who says, 'What happened to the old girl? Is she sick? Is she in the hospital? Did anybody see an ambulance? Or, did she finally just get fed up with her husband and walk out on him? And where'd she go? Holy shit, Mavis! Maybe she's dead.'"

This monolog got a laugh from the gathering, which counted among its number Hap, Maury, the inevitable Kenny and an appearance by Mose Irons, the town's barber and resident philosopher.

"I've seen my share of ... what's the term? Gone girls? ... in Hercules," offered Mose. "Wives who disappeared. Every time that happened, word got out, people started asking questions and pretty soon, the solution to the mystery was marital strife. Half the time, the women came back, none of 'em real happy with their situation but more or less resigned to it. Starting up a new life, from scratch, out there in the world tends to be harder—for a woman pushing fifty years, or sixty—than sticking it out with that unshaved slob on the couch in front of the TV with a beer can in his fist."

"Mose," said Crystal, who was parodying Carmen Miranda in a scoop-neck puffy-sleeve peasant blouse atop a hip-hugging silver lamé skirt slit to the thigh (sans the fruity headgear), "you're gonna make me cry."

"I can see what Mose is talkin' about," said Hap. "Elvira kept comin' back, but she finally decides, nope. She's not gonna take it anymore. So, she hops the bus and says, "Sayonara, Hercules!"

"Or," said Crystal, "she died."

"Yeah, maybe she kicked the bucket," said Maury, "right up there above the S&Q, and Pyramid Purlew didn't tell anybody, 'cause the one thing he wanted most in life, his dream come true, was a fresh dead body."

"Maury, aren't you going a little overboard?" said A.J., without much conviction.

"Am I?" retorted Maury. "What about all those dogs and cats that went missing ... and pigs! Minnie looked it up. She thinks Purlew was makin' mummies."

Otis tried to steer away from this line of speculation. "It's more like Minnie implied that ..."

Crystal leaned in. "Maury, you think Purlew could have actually turned Elvira into—"

"Oh, c'mon, Crys!" replied Maury. "Everybody was thinkin' it, even back then. And now, we've found four jars full of human organs up in Pyramid's attic."

Otis objected, evenly. "Maury, we don't know what's in those jars."

"That's 'cause you won't open 'em up!"

"Maury, we don't even know if Purlew put those jars up there. We can't connect him to those jars, or anything else in that apartment. There were probably a hundred different tenants there over the years. Speaking of years, A.J., how long's it been since anybody's seen Purlew, or his wife, in Hercules?"

"Hm, well, lemme think. The building was condemned and closed up about twenty years ago. I'd guess the last time anybody saw either of them was ten years ago," said A.J. "Probably longer than that for Elvira."

"Well then," said Otis. "I declare the case cold. A.J., I'm due one more beer."

"Wait a minute!" said Kenny, in a voice without a slur. "What about Orlo?"

"Oh, for Christ's sake," said Otis.

Carol, recalling previous citations of Orlo, filled in Hap on Pyramid Purlew's apparent barroom bromance with the amateur taxidermist.

"So," said Otis, grumpily, "what about Orlo? He's probably dead by now, or playing with his lips in a nursing home."

"No, n-no, he's alive," said Kenny, without any evidence.

"How do you know that, Kenny?" asked Crystal.

Kenny paused to sniff the fumes from his empty tumbler. "Can feel it," he said. "His spirit."

Kenny lifted the glass and waved it at A.J. "Speakin' of spirits ..."

A.J., ready with a bottle of vodka, refilled Kenny's glass. Kenny slurped half of it down and concluded, "Orlo's spiri's 'mong us. Feel it."

Exhausted by a moment of clarity, Kenny slipped into a light doze.

"Well, according to our favorite drunk," said Crystal, rubbing Kenny's head gently, "Orlo Bewick, who was the only friend Pyramid Purlew ever had, is alive, at least in spirit. Where'd you say, Carol?"

"I didn't."

"La Valle," said Mose.

"If he's alive," said Carol.

"He's not," snapped Otis.

Carol continued, unbowed. "But if he is, he might shed a little light on whatever became of Pyramid Purlew ... and Elvira."

"He might even know what it was lurking in that wreck of a building that scared the hell out of all those little kids," said Crystal.

This quieted everyone. They all took a drink. A.J. wiped the bar.

"Goddammit," said Maury, shattering the peace. "Can't somebody just drive to fuckin' La Valle?"

Otis lowered his head. "Christ," he said softly.

CHAPTER 25

(Wednesday, the 18th of June)

Otis held out a hand to the dog, a lanky mongrel with the resentful aspect of a jackal blackballed from the pack. The dog growled irresolutely and then tolerated a scratch behind the ear. The dog was lying beside a plastic chair that strained beneath the weight of Orlo Bewick, whose inert form could have been dead, save for the evenly spaced hisses of air coming from a pocked and purpled nose.

"So, you're not dead," said Otis, just above a whisper. "But are you coherent?"

"Sharp," came a voice from the figure in the plastic chair, "as I was before you were even a fuckin' pup."

With this, two small black pupils, edged with yellow, appeared between the florid folds and creases that constituted Orlo's face. While the body did not stir, the dark beads beneath two wildly flourishing white eyebrows gave Otis a lively once-over.

"Police?"

"That's right."

Orlo sat up. He was in flannels and khaki chinos, neither recently washed. He could have been eighty years old or a hard-used sixty. The only hair on his head was nine inches back from his eyebrows and tied up in a greasy gray-white ponytail.

"I know both the cops in this town. You're neither of 'em," said Orlo. "Where ya from? And whaddya want with me?"

Otis was in no hurry to explain himself. Entering the property, he had passed an ancient Ford-150 with rusted fringes and a floor panel in its bed that was bloodstained and redolent of dried offal. Orlo's precarious chair stood beside a plastic table strewn with beer cans and Twinkies wrappers. There was an ashtray spilling over with butts. Behind the alleged deer butcher was the relict of a filling station. Its prolonged disuse was indicated by the dirt on the siding, two broken windows patched with cardboard and a screen door from which most of the screen hung like the tongue of a deceased deer. Beneath the building's roofline was a weathered sign declaring that it contained someone who butchered deer. A hand-painted addendum on the signboard read "LOCKER PLANT."

There was also a garage without windows, its bay doors pulled down and padlocked.

"Orlo Bewick?"

Orlo looked up but didn't answer.

"I'd heard you retired from the venison business."

Orlo heaved himself from the chair, causing the dog to shift its weight several inches.

"Well, I don't do it regular anymore," said Orlo. "But if it's somebody I know and they want the buck's head on a plaque, well ..."

A dull hum from behind the building told Otis that Orlo's locker plant was still refrigerating.

"Must be the only locker plant in the county," he said amiably.

"That it is, but it's full," said Orlo, warming to the chance to talk business. "You'd be surprised how many folks don't have a proper deep-freeze at home."

Otis was finished with small talk. He said, "Orlo, I'm told you were the only friend that Francis Purlew had on God's whole earth."

"Francis who?"

Otis tapped Orlo hard enough on his chest to set him back a step. The dog watched this with interest. "Pyramid Purlew. You drank with him at the Roost."

Orlo raised an eyebrow a millimeter. "I've heard about you," he said. "You're the new cop in Hercules, ain'tcha?"

Otis nodded.

"I didn't call him Pyramid, or Francis," said Orlo, shedding his rural reticence. "He was Frank t'me."

"All right," said Otis. "I have a few questions."

Orlo nodded. "Sounds like a long talk."

"Possibly."

"Tell ya what," said Orlo. "I live out back of here. I'll go put on a clean shirt and meetcha over to the Roost in a while. You can buy me a beer or two, and I'll ..."

"Reminisce."

"Yeah, reminisce." Orlo smiled at that.

"An hour?"

Orlo nodded and started shuffling away. The dog, although visibly annoyed, followed.

CHAPTER 26

Carol had never been to the Red Rooster, the notorious roadhouse east of Hercules on Highway 33. So, when Otis called and told her he'd be late coming home, she asked why. He said he was meeting Orlo Bewick there to discuss his relationship with Pyramid Purlew. Carol said, "Ooh, that sounds really interesting. And do you know? I've never been to the Roost."

"Well, there's good reason for that," said Otis. "I wouldn't want you—"

Carol was beside Otis at the bar, at the Red Rooster, when Orlo shuffled in. He brightened almost comically at the sight of a woman beside the local police.

"Hiya, marshal. Who's she?"

"Never mind."

Carol introduced herself and shook Orlo's hand.

"Glad I put on a clean shirt," said Orlo.

Carol had convinced Stan, the Roost's proprietor, to uncork his only bottle of New Zealand sauvignon blanc. Otis was thankful that Stan had a Lakefront IPA on tap. Orlo chose the stool beside Carol, away from Otis, and ordered a shot of Jack and a pint of PBR. After drinking off a third of the beer, he dropped the shot into the glass. The fluid level rose to the brim but did not spill.

“Ah,” he said, pleased with his creation. He sipped at it delicately and smiled at Carol.

Otis needed the man’s attention. “You didn’t bring your dog,” he said.

“Dogs ain’t allowed in here,” replied Orlo, still enjoying the sight of Carol. “You oughta know that, marshal.”

“Call him Chief Otis,” Carol suggested.

“Chief Otis it is.”

“What’s his name?” Otis asked.

“Whose name?”

“The dog.”

Orlo finally turned toward Otis. “I call him Dog.”

“Original.”

“I’m gonna stuff ’im when he dies.”

“Really?” asked Carol, seemingly fascinated.

“Won’t be long,” said Orlo. “He’s old and he tends t’cough stuff up.”

“What stuff?”

“I don’t study it too careful, lady. I just flush it.”

“Ah.”

Carol’s presence was cramping Otis’ interrogatory style. He strove to seize the momentum.

“Orlo,” he said, “let’s talk about Pyramid Purlew.”

“Frank,” retorted Orlo.

“Right. You met him here?”

“Yeah, I did.”

“And you told him about your hobby?”

“What hobby?”

“Well,” said Otis, “taxidermy. You stuff—”

“It ain’t no hobby, cop. It’s my calling.”

“Oh. Right.”

“I’m goddamn good at it,” said Orlo. “I’m self-taught. I’m a fuckin’ artist.”

Orlo looked at Carol, suddenly penitent. "Sorry, miss. I didn't ..."

"It's okay," said Carol. "I know many words. I teach high school."

"Oh, you're a schoolteacher. That's really good. I always—"

"Excuse me," Otis broke in. "Purlew—Frank. You say he was interested in taxidermy?"

"I didn' say," said Orlo. "Tell ya the truth, he was more interested in dead things, in general. I guess you could say we had corpses in common."

Carol interrupted. "Corpses in common," she said, clutching Orlo's arm. "That would be a great name for a rock band."

Orlo grinned crookedly. "Yeah, it would, would'n'it?"

"Please," Otis tried again. "Can we just ..."

"Sorry, Chief," said Carol. "Press on."

Otis pressed on. "Orlo, about twenty years ago, according to our records, there was a rash of dogs and cats—and other animals—disappearing in Hercules. I don't know if you remember—"

"Course, I remember," said Orlo. "Frank needed 'em to practice on."

"He told you he was kidnapping people's pets?"

"Yeah, and pigs, too," said Orlo. "But the cop in Hercules, Big Knute somethin'."

"Nate Neitzel. He was my predecessor."

"Well, Frank figured Big ... er, Nate was on to him. Night I first talked to 'im, he figured he was goin' t'jail," said Orlo. "And I said to 'im I could give 'im all the fresh carcasses he needed, long as he didn't mind workin' on coons and possums. N'then, when I told 'im I could pick 'im up a deer or two, he got pretty excited. Y'see, a deer's pretty much the same size and weight as a human."

Otis knew the answer to his next question, but he asked

anyway. “Why did Purlew—Frank—want all these dead animals?”

“For mummies, silly,” said Carol.

“Yeah, mummies,” said Orlo. “He had, whaddyacallit, a sort of labertory.”

“Where?” asked Otis. “In the apartment on Main Street?”

“No, he couldn’t do that kinda work up there. He had a place up in the woods.”

“Where?”

“Up in the woods.”

“Which woods?”

“Search me,” said Orlo. “He’d pick me up, drive me there, and then he’d drive me back. It was dark. I don’ know where the hell—”

“You went there?” Otis was almost excited. “How often?”

“Lotsa times. I’d let Frank know I had a fresh carcass, no busted bones, all the guts still inside. He’d come get me, lickety split,” said Orlo. “Hey, can I get another drink?”

“Sure.”

Stan served Orlo and refilled Carol’s wine. Otis sipped his IPA.

“So, you delivered roadkill to Frank,” Otis said. “And then?”

“Well, that’s the thing. He coulda drove me home right away. He did the first couple times. But then, he asked could I stick around, maybe help ’im out. Course, I said, why not? It ain’t like I had anything else on my dance card, y’know?”

“So, you helped him out?”

“Yup.”

“Doing what?”

“Makin’ mummies.”

“From raccoons?”

“Yeah, and possums. I got ’im a fox once. A nice one. The critter’d stuck his nose out in traffic, got clipped on the head. Dead as bootnail, but the rest of ’im was perfect. Not mushed up or mangled at all. I would've stuffed that fox myself, but Frank, well, he gave me a hundred bucks for 'im."

"And he mummified it?" asked Carol.

"Oh yeah. I actually helped. Frank wanted me to learn how."

"He taught you how to make mummies?" asked Otis.

"Well, he tried."

"Why?"

"Search me," said Orlo. "Y'know what I think?"

"What do you think?" asked Carol.

"I think he just wanted a friend," said Orlo, almost sensitively. "I mean, nobody liked ol' Frank. I didn't like him much myself. But, pissy as ol' Frank was, we had this bond. I mean, it's kind of hard to find someone you can talk to about roadkill and all."

"I can see that," said Otis. "It's a pretty rare specialty."

"Fuckin' A," said Orlo, who immediately looked to Carol and added, "Oops."

She shrugged it off and asked, "So, how did the mummy lessons go?"

Orlo lowered his eyes and looked into his glass. "I guess you could say I'm a slow learner," he said. "I sorta got the hang of it, but Jesus ..."

"It's a complicated process," said Carol.

"Ya got that right, lady," replied Orlo.

"Please, call me Carol."

"Oh ... okay." The red of Orlo's face turned briefly redder.

Carol pressed on, informed by Natalie's mummy lore. "You have to start by taking out all the internal organs. Except the heart. Right, Orlo?"

"Yeah ... Carol," said Orlo. "Ya gotta have heart."

Carol smiled and chucked Orlo on the arm. He blushed again.

"Jesus," Otis whispered.

Orlo and Carol ran the gamut of mummification, starting with the coating of the body cavity and continuing to the sealing of the exterior with a preservative substance.

"Frank used honey," said Orlo.

"Really?"

"Yeah, there's a beekeeper over in Hercules."

"I know him," said Otis.

"The thing that bothered Frank, when I brought him critters from the woods, raccoons 'n' all, he didn't like the fur."

"The fur?" asked Carol. "Why?"

"Well, Carol," said Orlo, intimately. "A good mummy's gotta be clean. I mean, like, spotless. And fur's a pain in the ass. It picks up fleas 'n' ticks 'n' all kindsa cooties. You got dirt, pine needles, dried blood stuck in amongst all the hairs, and whaddya gonna do? It ain't like you could just shave a possum, y'know."

"You couldn't?"

"Jeez no, it's messy as hell. Don't even try it."

"I won't," said Carol.

"Once, Frank tried scorchin' the fur off a coon with a propane torch. Jesus Christ."

"What happened?"

"Christ, it was like a bonfire of old tires covered with shit. The smell almost killed us. We had t'go outside for an hour. My clothes smelled like dead burnt coon for a month, 'til I finally got around to washin' 'em."

Carol reserved comment on Orlo's laundry schedule.

"So, anyhow, Frank ended up usin' pine resin," said Orlo. "Gave up tryin' to scrape or burn off the goddamn fur, just left it on the carcass and smeared it all over with that sticky shit. He said the Egyptians used it, way back when. Said it keeps things forever."

"Oh, we knew that," said Carol. "We have an expert."

Orlo rolled on. "Frank kept saying he'd love it if I brought him a pig. They're pretty hairless. Thing is, you don't find a whole lot of dead hogs alongside the Interstate."

"Orlo, it seems as though you've got the details down pat. I bet you could make a mummy."

"No, ma'am. Nope," said Orlo. "If I even tried, I'd do somethin' too soon, or not soon enough, or I'd do the steps out of order and end up with nothin' but a stinkin' mess of bones 'n' innards."

Otis intervened. "So, Orlo, that was quite a while ago."

Orlo answered Otis more cautiously than he did with Carol. "What was?"

"Your friendship with Frank."

"Oh yeah. Years."

"When's the last time you saw him?"

Orlo took a long pull on his second depth charge. "Well then, jeez ..."

"He must've been still living in Hercules then? Upstairs from the S&Q Hardware?"

Orlo paused before answering, laboring to look thoughtful. "Yup. As I recall. That's about right."

"With Elvira?"

"Yup."

"How well did you know Elvira?"

"Elvira? No. Not at all."

"Never met her?"

"Nope."

"Don't know what became of her?"

Orlo twitched. "Whaddya mean?"

"Like you said, Orlo, Purlew was not a likable fella, apparently even with his wife," said Otis. "Elvira could only stand him for a certain period of time and then she just had to get away. You must've known about that? About her taking off to stay with her relatives?"

"Oh, well, I guess, yeah," said Orlo. "Frank mighta mentioned it."

"Right," said Otis. "The general thinking is that she finally got fed up with Frank for good, took off and—that time—she never came back."

Orlo had no comment.

"But that would've been later, right?"

"Elvira was still with Frank," added Carol, "the last time you saw him?"

Orlo nodded.

"So you wouldn't have the foggiest notion whatever became of Elvira?"

Orlo was silent.

"Would you, Orlo?"

"Oh. Nope," said Orlo, somewhat evasively, to his beer.

"Or, for that matter," added Otis, "whatever became of Pyramid Purlew himself?"

Orlo took a firm two-handed grip on his glass. "Nope," he said.

"Not a clue?"

"Nope."

Otis and Carol both peered intently at Orlo, who shunned eye contact.

After a while, Carol broke the tension. "How about," she said to Otis, "you and I try out that new restaurant over in Hillsboro? I skipped lunch today, and I'm starving."

Otis caught the hint. "Yeah, I guess we should go."

He nudged Orlo. "Thanks for the help, Mr. Bewick," he said, formally.

"Oh, don' mention it," Orlo mumbled.

Otis settled the check and headed out of the Roost. In the parking lot, Carol said, "Wow."

"Wow what?"

Carol smiled. "Orlo's got a secret."

"Well, seems like he's gonna keep it," said Otis.

"You're just giving up, like that?" Carol snapped her fingers. "You're a Chicago detective. Don't you want to know?"

"Know what?"

"Whatever became of Pyramid Purlew. And Elvira."

"This ain't Chicago, babe. Detecting's a lot more complicated out here in the middle of nowhere. I've got no forensics, no databases. Instead of confidential informants, all I have is a town full of gossips. I don't even have a partner."

"You have me," said Carol.

"Well, that's my consolation." Otis kissed her submissively.

Carol persisted. "You must be curious. You're always curious."

"I am, but this whole thing has all the signs of a dead end."

"The dead at the end might be a mummy."

"Clever."

"Look, Fosdick. Somewhere around here is Purlew's mummy lab. Orlo was there. He saw it. It can't be far. It holds the secret."

"What secret?"

"If we knew, it wouldn't be a secret, Fosdick."

Otis sighed and spread his arms. "It's in the woods, toots. I'm from Chi. You're from Madison. Neither of us is exactly Davy Crockett. And Orlo's no help. He's been there a dozen times and he has no idea where it is."

"I think he does," said Carol.

"Well, he's not telling."

"Somebody else must know."

"Even if someone did know, and even if we found the place, what's the point?"

"The point, Fosdick? The point is 'What if?'"

"What if what?"

"That's exactly my point!" said Carol, with the sort of finality that bristled with unfinished business.

"Are you really hungry?" Otis asked defeatedly.

"Starved."

"Okay then, Nancy Drew. Let's go eat."

CHAPTER 27

(Thursday, the 19th of June)

Otis' stool at A'Jay's had become a hot seat. He had arrived with expectations of celebrating Teddy Gilbert's official criminology degree from the technical college over in Fennimore. But no sooner had Teddy blown out the candles on a cake baked by A.J.'s wife, Kiayla, than he turned on Otis and asked, "What's goin' on with you, Chief?"

Otis greeted this with a stare as blank as he could muster. But the curiosity of a whole barful of barflies bore in on him.

"Yeah," said Crystal, wearing a maroon tuxedo and matching velvet top hat in honor of Teddy. "You're off your feed. Jimmy. I mean, we can all understand your deciding to put off the wedding and move in with Carol. You're lookin' before you leap. But now you're dithering over this business with Pyramid Purlew and the curse of the Kuckuck sisters. This is juicy stuff, Jimmy. Everybody's wondering about it, but you just keep sayin' there's nothin' to see here. Whatever happened to the crime-fightin' bulldog of Hercules PD?"

Otis' response was a puzzled scowl.

"I know what's eating the guy," said A.J., as he delivered Otis a black and tan.

Otis sipped his beer and peered warningly at A.J., who ignored the warning.

"He's distracted," said A.J.

"Distracted?" asked Crystal. "By what?"

"He's got a case of Josie Dobbs Flu," he said.

A.J. leaned into Otis' face and said. "She's on his mind. She's in his blood. She upsets his stomach, and she keeps him awake nights." He winked at Carol. "Doesn't he?"

"Well, he's not sleeping well," she confirmed.

"Ever since that little girl plugged James in the leg and wafted off into an ill wind," said A.J.

"Sheer poetry," said Carol, squeezing A.J.'s hand.

"Aw, shucks," said A.J.

"By Jove," said Maury. "I think he's got it."

"Course he's right," said Hap. "That gorgeous little devil's been pushin' the chief's buttons ever since he first got to town. Ain't that right, Chief?"

Otis chose not to honor this charge with a reply.

While Crystal and company went on ragging Otis for his complacency about the mysterious jars in Pyramid Purlew's attic and the secret laboratory in the forest primeval, A.J. was scribbling on a cocktail napkin. A break in the conversation afforded him an opening to sing the reprise of a blues lyric scrawled illegibly on the napkin. His voice was a rich baritone, reminiscent of Levi Stubbs.

"Oh, Josie, Josie," he sang.

He paused.

Crystal brightened. "Is there more?"

"Oh yeah," said A.J.

"Please," said Otis softly, "don't."

"Let 'er rip, Aje!" insisted Crystal.

"Yes!" said Carol, betraying her fiancé.

A.J. let 'er rip.

"Josie," he crooned, *"oh Josie,*

"Josie, Josie Dobbs!

"She smiles, she flirts,

"She murders and robs."

"Oh, that's good," said Hap.

"No, it's not," muttered Otis.

A.J. sang on.

"Chief Otis gets up with that gal on his mind,

"Oh, Jim Otis gets up, and she's on his mind.

"But Josie's ahead, Jimmy's always behind."

This brought a shout of approval from everyone but Otis.

"Oh, she shot Frankie dead in the Mad City woods,

"That gal plugged Frank in them deep dark woods.

"Jim went there to catch her, dead sure that he could."

At this point, Stewy McCullough, Hercules High basketball star, who had dropped in with his girlfriend Meryl Clark (they were both drinking ginger ale), caught up with A.J.'s flow and started to hum a little harmony.

"But sweet Josie Dobbs, she could handle a gun,

"Our Josie saw Jimmy and leveled her gun.

"She broke Jimmy's leg 'n' took off on the run.

"Josie, oh Josie,

"Our sweet Josie Dobbs,

"She's blonde and she's lovely,

"She kills and she robs."

A.J. repeated the refrain, with Stewy in duet. A third reprise brought in Meryl, Carol, Crystal, Hap, Teddy, FBI agent Tyrone Thrush and even Kenny.

One more rendition involved half the patrons in A'Jay's, some of whom—GIs from Fort McCoy—had no idea who Josie Dobbs was. But they were drunk.

"Jesus Christ," mumbled Otis.

A.J. had to break off his recital to serve an influx of drinkers, leaving Otis in a sour funk with an empty glass. "I almost had her, y'know. If she hadn't …"

Otis didn't finish the sentence.

Teddy intervened. "Hey, Chief, look. It's out of your hands, right? We sent her picture out to every police force in four states. She's gone from here anyhow, Chief. As long as you're in Hercules, she can't come home."

"First of all, Teddy," said Otis, "the photo we sent was a copy of her high-school yearbook picture. You really think she still looks like that?"

"Well ..."

"And even if they caught her," Otis pressed on, "what the hell they gonna charge her with? The day she shot me, I never laid eyes on her. They took a bullet out of my leg, but they've got no gun to compare the ballistics. That vicious little bitch has committed, Christ, how many crimes, and I don't have a fucking shred—"

"The point is, Fosdick," said Carol, aborting Otis' soliloquy, "she's not here. Probably not coming back. She's not your problem."

"She's always my problem," growled Otis.

"No," said Carol, "Crys is right."

"I am?" asked Crystal.

"About what?" demanded Otis.

"About this Purlew business," said Carol. "Two people disappeared from this town and—"

"Goddammit," said Otis. "People move all the time. They leave towns like this and they never come back. That's not a mystery. It's just ... moving."

"But what about Elvira?" asked Carol. "She leaves all of a sudden."

"Probably to Reno, to get a divorce," said Otis. "You heard what Orlo said. Purlew was impossible to live with. Elvira moves out. A while later, her husband moves out. Maybe he went looking for her. Maybe he got lonely."

"Talk about bullshit," observed Kenny.

"No, no, no, Jimmy," said Crystal. "You can't get away with that. Purlew and his wife didn't just up and move out. She vanished. Then he vanished. People who just move out don't leave behind a haunted building that scared the hell out of half the little kids in town and even spooked the town's Ho-Chunk witch doctor. And they don't leave behind four huge jars full of God knows what, which might be some sort of human remains. And you just sit here feelin' sorry for yourself? This ain't the Jimmy Otis I know and love!"

"And what if he's still around?" asked Carol. "You heard Orlo. There's some sort of hideout up in the woods. What if Pyramid Purlew is still alive?"

"What if he's diggin' people out of their graves?" offered Hap.

"Oh, for Christ's sake," said Otis.

Meryl Clark spoke softly. "I think you should look for it, Chief."

"Look for what?"

"The hideout."

"Well, how—"

"You have to talk to Orlo again, Jim," said Carol.

"Orlo?"

"He didn't tell us everything he knows."

"Orlo?"

"C'mon, Fosdick," Carol said. "You've grilled a thousand suspects. You know when they're holding something back. I could tell that Orlo was holding back. The man's got a secret."

"And he's old," said Teddy.

"Old? Why does that—"

"Jeez, Chief. You don't want him to die with his secret, do ya?"

"What secret?"

"Well," said Crystal, "that's the whole point, isn't it, Jimmy? What secret?"

"Yeah, what secret?" said Hap.

Kenny chimed in. "What secret?"

CHAPTER 28

(Friday, the 20th of June)

Hercules town clerk Danielle Whelihan, who had majored in history at UW–Platteville, loved the village's dusty old ledgers. They were America's heritage in her hands. So, when Police Chief Jim Otis, looking vaguely beleaguered, came to her counter in the City Hall asking if there were any property records, perhaps twenty years old—or older—related to someone named Francis Purlew, she flashed an eager smile and dropped everything.

The City Hall basement was a labyrinth to most town employees but a refuge to Dani Whelihan, where she breathed air thick with memory. She could hide there from the pestering of Mayor Luke Winstead and from a telephone that never stopped ringing. She led the police chief downstairs, flicked on the second row of fluorescent lights above shelves stacked eight feet high with heavy ledgers.

"Holy smokes, Dani, I had no idea how much stuff there is to go through," said Otis, ready to forsake the goose chase.

"No, no, Chief, I know this dungeon like I know my kids' faces," said the clerk. "All I need to find anything down here is a time frame and the alphabet."

Otis offered a mid-1990s time frame, then helped Dani remove three of the heavy books from an upper shelf. She led the police chief to a broad table beneath the staircase. She flipped a switch on a blazing halogen bulb above the table. Almost before Otis had set the volumes onto the table, she was flipping pages dustily.

She turned to the back pages in the top book and ran her finger down a row of handwritten entries. "Nope, not in '94," she said.

She attacked the next ledger. "Every year, 'til 1999, we kept records of foundations built," said Dani.

"Uh huh," said Otis, struggling not to cough.

"But in '99, the council passed an ordinance against people living in a foundation with a roof on top."

"A dugout," said Otis.

"Yes, they decided it was dangerous, but the real issue, if you want to know, was the property taxes. If you just live in the cellar with no house above, your assessment is chump change, Chief."

"I see," said Otis. "So, since '99—"

"Well," Dani went on as she searched the back pages of the 1995 ledger, "they passed their ordinance against dugouts, but they never enforced it, because nobody ever got charged with a violation, because by then, nobody was living in dugouts anymore. Most folks nowadays don't even know what a dugout is. I had an uncle, up in Tomah, who barely had two nickels to rub. But he bought a cheap quarter-acre on the edge of town, dug out the cellar and built a foundation. He covered it with plywood sheets and asphalt shingles and moved the whole family underground. They lived like gophers for six years 'til my uncle could afford to put a house on top. But now, that sort of thing isn't possible, and it's not legal in most towns. Besides, in Hercules, it's cheaper to buy a double-wide and hope to God a tornado doesn't roll in."

This was more information than Otis had bargained for. "Yes, I see. Well—"

"Here it is!" Dani pointed, with a red fingernail dotted with black to evoke a ladybug, at a single cursive line atop a blank page, written in blue ink.

Otis was flummoxed, but there it was.

"17 October 1995," Dani recited. "Foundation dug, prospective house, two bedrooms. No value—that means the assessors hadn't gone out there yet, and probably never did."

"What's the location?" Otis asked.

"Right there, see?" said Dani. "Quarry Road, no street number. Chief, because it's not a street. It's just—"

"A trail in the woods."

"I guess," said Dani. "I've certainly never been up there."

Dani slammed the ledger shut.

"Are you going up there, Chief?"

"I guess I'll have to."

Dani smiled. "Will you tell me what you find?"

"I'm hoping not to find anything."

The town clerk tilted her head curiously.

"Thanks, Dani," said Otis. "I'll let you know."

The Bensonville quarry—named for a town that no longer existed—was inside the "city limits" of Hercules. All the good granite had been taken out of a great gouge in the earth forty years before. There wasn't a single living quarryman in town. The quarry was surrounded by woods and filled with water eighty feet deep. It was frequented by teenagers who came to either canoodle in parked cars or swim in water polluted by fluids seeping from the trucks, tractors and stolen cars that had been driven off the edge over the years. The quarry had claimed at least two lives, one a high school freshman who had dived in on a dare twenty years before. The other was Peter Yates, whom Josie Dobbs had goaded into trying to jump the quarry on a Harley-Davidson bike named Eloise.

Otis had been to the quarry too often since arriving in Hercules, almost always to deal with tragedy, the latest being the murder of Crystal MacDougal's misguided nephew, Billy Kneedler. To reach the alleged Quarry Road, Otis drove gingerly around the quarry on a never-used gravel road barely wide enough for his car.

Otis later learned, from A.J. Cartwright, that Quarry Road had been chewed out of the woods by a developer harboring hopes of a subdivision atop a glacial drumlin with views stretching south and west toward the Kickapoo River. The developer's dreams ended with a ruling by the state's historical agency that the drumlin was the likely site of a Ho-Chunk burial ground. As long as there might be dead Indigenous in the ground, nobody was allowed to erect houses on top of them.

This ruling, of course, rendered Francis Purlew's dugout also illegal. But his clandestine project had, in the timeless cliché of every bureaucracy since Babylon, "slipped through the cracks."

Driving Quarry Road, little more than a pair of tire ruts through knee-high weeds, Otis had to stop several times to move fallen limbs from his path. The climb got steep and violently rocky before suddenly leveling off into a clearing. Stepping out of the Bluesmobile, Otis could easily judge that everything there had been long abandoned. But it was undoubtedly the place where Pyramid Purlew had brought Orlo Bewick for mummification lessons.

Otis didn't want Minnie involved yet, so he bypassed the radio in his car and dialed Teddy.

"Teddy, you interested in a little overtime?"

Teddy laughed. "Course, Chief."

"Good. Get over to La Valle. Track down Orlo Bewick. I want him up here as fast as you can haul the son of a bitch."

"Up where, Chief?"

Otis began to explain his location, but Teddy broke in. He was a townie. "Oh, sure, Chief. Back of the quarry. I'll see you in a while."

While Otis was talking to Teddy, his eyes adjusted to the shade cast by the surrounding trees. There were two structures in the clearing, both half-concealed by a weedy overgrowth.

The cinder-block walls of Purlew's dugout were barely a foot higher than ground level. Purlew had covered the underground dwelling with a roof, slightly crowned and covered with asphalt shingles that appeared to be, after all those years, mostly intact.

The dugout's only entrance was a formidably solid door—secured with a dead bolt and a padlock—that intruders had battered but not breached. The age and nature of the intruders was indicated by the litter they had left behind: cigarette butts, bleached beer cans, pill bottles, a couple of drug vials and several shriveled condoms. There was also a ravaged t-shirt bearing the logo of the Milwaukee Brewers and a shoe that looked as though it had been under the weather for a decade.

Otis stifled the urge to look for the other shoe and returned to his car for a tire iron. He paused to study the other structure on Francis Purlew's secluded lot. It was a jumble of cube-cut stones, apparently gleaned from the quarry. The granite cubes had been laboriously hewn to match one another. From the pile of hand-cut blocks, several grayed and splintered four-by-four timbers jutted up.

It took Otis some effort and a bloody knuckle to pry open Purlew's dugout. He kicked at the door 'til it scraped inward. He hesitated, remembering his last experiences with a dark doorway into a hovel once occupied by Pyramid Purlew.

Otis took two steps inside and looked around. The interior was as lightless as a coal shaft. But the darkness was inert. Nothing rushed from the blackness to tear at Otis' flesh and unhinge his mind. He turned on a flashlight and stepped inside. The gloom was dense enough that Otis could only see within the circle of the flashlight beam. Save for a table bearing a kerosene lamp and a pair of rickety chairs, there was little furniture. A rudimentary kitchen, with an ancient Norge refrigerator and a hotplate, as well as a string of lightbulbs along the low-slung ceiling, hinted to Otis that Purlew had probably powered the place, long ago, with a gasoline generator. He had seen no sign of that device outside. The dominant feature of the space was a long, narrow hardwood slab, mounted on six heavy legs, suggesting an operating table in a hospital, or a morgue. He peered at the table surface, seeking signs of what Purlew had done there, but—except for a thick coat of dust—it was largely unblemished.

Penetrating deeper, Otis found evidence of the table's purpose. Lined along the back wall, neatly arranged in order of their size, from what was probably a chipmunk to what could only be a white-tail deer, likely a doe, were muslin-wrapped animal mummies. Among them, Otis could only guess, were squirrels and raccoons, opossums, a small pig and a creature that was either a dog or a coyote. Altogether, they gave off a slightly sweet odor, a little musty but not strong or fetid. They made Otis think of packages under a macabre Christmas tree.

He picked up a medium-size package and carried it over to Purlew's table. He swept away enough dust to lay down the object. Under the eerie glow from his flashlight, he took out his pocket knife and carefully cut away the wrappings. Inside was a raccoon, remarkably preserved, its fur matted with a thick fluid that had dried and hardened. Its face was lifelike, its jaws slightly open, revealing a row of small, sharp teeth turned yellow. Its limbs, clever little front paws and busy hind feet, were virtually unchanged since the creature's death. Otis probed an incision in the raccoon's side, and found—instead of entrails—a cotton sack, decayed by time and leaking a trickle of sawdust.

Otis felt an attack of the creeps coming on, so he left the mummified raccoon on the table and backed out of Purlew's dugout.

Emerging to notice that the light was failing, he felt his phone vibrate in his pocket.

"Hi, Chief, I was trying to call," said Teddy.

Otis guessed that phone reception was impossible in

Pyramid Purlew's underground mortuary. "Sorry, Teddy. What's up?"

"I'm over at La Valle. I found Mr. Bewick. Should I bring him—"

"Not here, Teddy. It's getting dark," said Otis. "Take him to Hercules, put him in a cell."

"In a cell?" asked Teddy, noticeably alarmed. "He's under arrest?"

"Yeah, let's see." Otis thought for a moment. "Yeah, for hindering an investigation."

"Really?"

"Yes! The old fart didn't tell us half of what he knew about Purlew."

"Okay, chief. What about, um, arraigning him?"

"Teddy, we just want to keep him overnight someplace where we can find him in the morning," said Otis.

"Well, okay." Teddy sounded dubious. Otis hung up.

Driving down Quarry Road, in the dark, was almost as creepy as unwrapping Pyramid Purlew's mummified raccoon.

CHAPTER 29

(Saturday, the 21st of June)

Before Otis could deal with Orlo Bewick, he had to meet the 10:30 bus from Chicago. When Natalie had learned that her father was on the track of a mummy—or mummies—she couldn't be kept away.

"Daddy, did you find an actual mummy?"

"Well ..."

"Where, where, where? I wanna see, I wanna see."

"Kid, be cool," said Otis, gently stroking his daughter's hair. "I'll take you along, but only if you stay in the background."

"Oh."

"Quietly."

Natalie's nod was insincere.

After a night in the Hercules lockup, Orlo was fractious. As soon as Maury brought him into Otis' office, he issued a threat. "I'm gonna get a fuckin' lawyer and I'm gonna eat your balls for lunch, motherfucker."

"Orlo Bewick," said Otis. "My daughter, Natalie."

Bewick paled visibly. "Oh, shit." He crouched and extended his hands penitently toward the girl. "I didn't mean ... I didn't see ... Look, sweetie, I'm sorry."

"Oh, don't worry, Mr. Bewick," said Natalie, bravely taking Orlo's unwashed hand. "I'm from Chicago."

Orlo, who seemed to accept this explanation, sighed with relief.

Otis broke in. "Orlo, I explained last night. You're not under arrest. You're more like a material witness, which is why I kept you here."

"Oh yeah?" said Orlo, straightening and regaining a measure of insouciance. "Witness to what?"

"That's what I mean to find out," said Otis. "And that's why we're going up Quarry Road, to Purlew's dugout."

"Quarry Road?"

"Sound familiar?"

"Er ..."

"Orlo, you knew all along where Purlew's hideout was, didn't you?"

"Well ..."

Before heading for the dugout in the woods, Otis made clear that he expected a complete account of Orlo's experience with Pyramid Purlew.

"Yeah, okay, that's ... okay," said Orlo, with the air of a man too long burdened by confidentiality.

Otis knew that Connie would be appalled that he was bringing his daughter to the scene of what might be either a crime or just a lot of ghoulish behavior by a weird old man. His alibi was that Natalie had established herself as the nearest available expert on ancient Egyptian funerary practices. Besides, Carol was coming along as Natalie's chaperone.

Otis said to Natalie, "You can't tell your mother about this."

Natalie rolled her eyes. "C'mon, Daddy. If I told Mom half the things I do with you, she'd never let me out of the house again."

With Orlo in his back seat, Maury followed Otis' car up Quarry Road.

It was still before noon when the two vehicles parked in Pyramid Purlew's clearing. It was larger than the Grove, but it exuded a similar air of illicit gloom. Maury unloaded Orlo, along with a half-dozen battery-operated camping lanterns.

Otis surveyed the scene once more and pointed to the pile of rubble beside Purlew's dugout.

"All right, Orlo. What's that?"

"Aw, well, that's Frank's pyramid, or it was," said Orlo. "Damn. Looks like it all caved in."

"Caved into what?" asked Otis.

"The burial chamber."

"Burial chamber? Something is buried there?"

"Hell, yeah," said Orlo. "Some*body*."

"Who?" asked Otis, dreading the answer.

"Elvira. Frank built it for her."

"Whoa," said Natalie softly.

Reflexively, Otis recalled the parting words of John Stormwalker: "Remove the body."

Otis turned on Orlo, planting a hand on his chest. "She was the body—in the Kuckuck building."

"What building?" asked Orlo evasively.

Otis took a grip on Orlo's shirt. "You helped him, didn't you?"

"Helped?"

"Yes, Orlo. *Helped.* Elvira was dead upstairs, wasn't she?"

"Yeah, well, uh ... she was dead when I got there."

"So, then, you and your friend, Frank Purlew, took Elvira's body down those steps and tossed her into the back of your truck, didn't you?"

"I toldja, Frank wasn't no friend."

"Fine. But you helped him remove the body."

"Well, yeah. Frank couldn't've done it by himself, not down those stairs. Elvira wasn't heavy but, y'know, she was dead. She sort of flopped around. And those stairs were steep, slippery, and it was dark. We had t'wait 'til after midnight so nobody'd see."

Otis shook his head. "And then you drove her up here."

"Nope," said Orlo, firmly. "Didn' do that."

Otis hadn't expected this answer. "So, did you help Purlew move his wife's body or didn't you?"

"Yeah, I jis' said so," said Orlo. He paused to snork something up from his throat and spit it out. "But we didn't bring 'er here."

"You didn't bring her here?"

"Nope."

"Where'd you bring her?" Natalie asked, bursting with curiosity.

Orlo leaned down and talked gently to the girl. "Over t'my place, honey."

"To your place?" asked Otis.

"'T's right," said Orlo, with an odd touch of pride. "We wrapped 'er up in butcher paper and put 'er in my locker plant. She got a whole shelf all to 'erself."

"You froze Elvira?" asked Otis.

Carol giggled. Natalie said, "Wow! Really?"

Otis said, "Why in God's name would you do that?"

"Why?" said Orlo. "Jeez Christ, we had to. The pyramid wasn't finished."

This explanation, logical though it sounded, triggered a moment of stunned silence.

Orlo filled the gap. "Yeah, ol' Frank, he'd dug out Elvira's tomb. He laid the floor, painted the walls and all. He had the timbers laid on top—I had t'help 'im with that. But he was still cuttin' the stone. So, we stored Elvira over t'my place."

"You froze the body of a dead woman?" said Otis flatly.

"Had to, if Frank was gonna make 'er into a mummy," said Orlo. "Y'know, I think he prob'ly liked my freezer more'n he liked me."

Otis considered this and said, "You didn't need a lawyer before, Orlo," said Otis. "Now, you do."

"Why? Wha'd I do?"

Forgoing any further dialog with Orlo, Otis shoved him toward the dugout. Following closely, Maury distributed the lanterns, lending the cellar the atmosphere of a well-lit mausoleum. Pools of light revealed the shapes of animals encased in layers of fabric in a mixture of colors and patterns.

Otis pushed Orlo over to the "operating table" that dominated the dugout's interior. He faced Orlo across the table. One of Maury's lanterns illuminated half of Orlo's face, leaving the other half in shadow. Orlo was still trying to present a facade of stern defiance, but his eyes and trembling lips betrayed his guilt and anxiety.

"How long did you keep Elvira in cold storage, Orlo?"

"Oh, a year or so, I s'pose."

"Uh huh. So, after the pyramid was built," said Otis, "you put her in the back of your truck and brought her here? You laid Elvira out on this table?"

"Yeah, yeah, right here."

"And Frank went to work mummifying Elvira?"

"No," said Orlo, "we had t'let 'er thaw first. It took a coupla days."

"Wait," Carol broke in. "When did this happen? When did Elvira die?"

"When Elvira died? Uh, lemme think," said Orlo. He rubbed his head. "Hell, must've been twenty years ago."

Otis shook his head. "Elvira's been dead twenty years, and nobody knew?" he said. "Except you, Orlo?"

"Well, it ain't like Frank coulda told anybody."

Otis' voice roared. "Why the hell not?"

Natalie butted back in. "Oh, I know."

Otis turned toward his daughter, but before he could tell her to be quiet, she was talking to Orlo. "Mr. Bewick, you said he was going to mummify Elvira, didn't you?"

Orlo looked at the girl, surprised. "Well, yeah, honey. He was—"

"Mr. Bewick," said Natalie. "Mr. Purlew wanted to prepare Elvira for the afterlife, didn't he?"

"That's right, honey. That's why—"

"That's why," Natalie piped up triumphantly, "Purlew couldn't tell anybody Elvira was dead. They'd take the body and bury her and she'd never be a mummy, and she'd just be plain old dead. No afterlife, Daddy."

As often occurred with Natalie, Otis felt bushwhacked. "I see," he said.

While her father organized his thoughts, Natalie continued the interrogation. "Mr. Bewick, you said—"

"Hey, hon, call me Orlo."

"Okay, Orlo, but don't call me 'honey.' My name is Natalie."

Otis caught Carol's eye. She smiled.

"Orlo," said Natalie. "When you brought Elvira here, there were parts of her that were missing, right?"

"Parts?" said Maury.

"Y're darn right, Natalie," said Orlo, warming to the girl's style. "The first thing after Elvira passed, even before Frank called me to help him move the body, Jesus. He'd cut her open—on the goddamn kitchen table—and took out most of her innards. You shoulda seen the mess on the kitchen floor."

"Orlo, y'see, he had to do that," said Natalie, "because those soft organs in the body, they rot really fast. That's why the Egyptians cut them out when the body was almost still warm, and put them into canopic jars, in embalming juice."

"Thanks, Nat," said Otis, struggling to regain control. "What next, Orlo?"

"Look, Chief," pled Orlo, " I didn't wanna be here. I helped the crazy sumbitch haul Elvira up here. I thought that was all. I said, 'I'm outa here, Frank.' But he wouldn't let me go. He made me watch."

"Good. So, you watched," said Otis. "What did you see?"

Orlo exhaled wearily. "Awright, well, next thing he did, he spent a long time wiping out Elvira's insides, with rags and alcohol, from her neck all the way down to her ... um, crotch. When he was done, she was clean as a whistle. I tell ya, Chief, you could've ate offa Elvira's ribcage, on the inside of it."

"Ew," said Carol, involuntarily.

"Welcome to Golden Corral," said Maury, snickering.

"And then?" Otis pressed.

"Yeah, right," said Orlo. "And then, he had this big canister of stuff. I think he called it neutron."

"Natron," said Natalie. "It's a mixture of salts—sodium bicarbonate, sodium sulfate, sodium—"

"We got it, Nat. Thanks," said Otis. "Orlo?"

"Well then, Frank jist, like, painted the whole inside of Elvira with this neut ... er, nate—"

"Natron," said Natalie. "It dries out the tissues and preserves them. It's pretty cool!"

"But then ..." Orlo paused. "I really hated this part."

"The brain, right?" said Natalie.

"You know about that?" Orlo asked.

"Oh, of course!" crowed Natalie. "Y'see, Orlo, the Egyptians thought the heart was where you had all your feelings and did all your thinking. They thought the brain was just sort of a big dumb sponge inside your head. And they had to get it out of there because it would start to putrefy and ruin the mummy."

"Izzat right?" said Orlo, knitting his brow. "Frank never told me 'bout that."

"Orlo," said Otis, with a note of impatience, "what did he do?"

"With Elvira's brains?"

"Yes, with her brain."

Orlo winced at the memory. "Awright, so he takes this rat-tail wire brush with this long handle and then, before I can look away, he shoves it right up Elvira's nose. And it gets stuck. So, Frank pushes hard and there's this sort of squishy pop. And the wire brush goes right up inside Elvira's ... skull."

"That's right, Orlo," said Natalie, encouragingly. "That's how the Egyptians did. Except they heated the poker, which helped to sort of melt the brain."

"Lovely," said Carol.

"And Frank, he takes, oh, I don' know, five minutes rootin' around in Elvira's head. I could hear that rat-tail scrape on the bone. But that wasn't the worst part."

Natalie assisted. "He turned Elvira's brain into a lot of loose mush, like soup."

"Yeah," said Orlo. "Brain soup."

"That's right, Orlo. But once it was liquefied, he still had to get it out," said Natalie. "What did he use?"

Orlo was catching Natalie's excitement. "He had a machine," he said to Natalie. "This suction thing. He bought it from some hospital supply outfit. So he pulled out the wire brush and he shoved a tube up Elvira's nose again and turned on that machine. And there it came, pumpin' out of Elvira's skull."

"Brain soup," said Natalie, with inordinate gratification.

"Brain soup," Orlo confirmed.

"Oh my God," whispered Carol.

"Course, it clogged a couple of times, when these big chunks came out—"

"That's enough on the brains, Orlo," said Otis. "What next?"

"Oh, right," said Orlo. "Frank popped out Elvira's eyeballs."

"Oh, God!" said Carol.

"I think I need to leave the room," said Maury.

"I told Frank I'd give 'im a couple of the fake eyeballs I use when I stuff deer," said Orlo.

"Fine," said Otis. "Move on."

"Well, then, we washed her. Head to toe."

"This is a really important part of the ritual," said Natalie. "In a mummy, purity is everything."

"Thanks, kid," said Otis.

"And we dried her," said Orlo, "And then the paint job."

"Paint job?" asked Otis.

"Oh, cool!" said Natalie. "What did you use, Orlo?"

"Frank had a couple gallons of pine tar, the red kind."

"Oh, yes," said Natalie. "Red would be right. And you coated her with it."

"Yup."

"You see, Daddy, the pine resin keeps air away from the skin and muscle, so it doesn't decay. It keeps out bugs and cooties and flies and microbes. Everything."

"I see."

"And then," said Natalie to Orlo, "you wrapped her."

"That's right, honey—er, Natalie. Frank had a pile of old clothes he'd bought over t'the Goodwill in La Crosse. Or he might've stolen 'em. He'd tore 'em all into long strips. I swear we were damn near two hours wrappin' up Elvira."

"And that was it?"

"Oh no, Daddy," said Natalie. "A mummy has to, like, cure, for at least forty days. And then, you unwrap her, and you fill the body cavity and the skull with, like stuffing."

"Like a Thanksgiving turkey?" asked Maury, who had not left after all.

Natalie glared at him.

"Sorry."

"The Egyptians used linen and sawdust and other material," Natalie continued. "And then, finally, the mummy got re-wrapped all over again, with another coat of pine resin, or cedar oil or this black stuff, bitumen."

"Frank used honey," said Orlo.

"Really?" said Natalie. "Honey?"

"Yeah."

"Cool."

"Yeah, cool," said Orlo. He smiled gappily at the girl.

"Anyway, Orlo, you see. Then, the mummy's ready to face the forty-two questions from the forty-two judges and try to find eternal life on the Field of Reeds."

"Cool," said Orlo again.

Otis leaned in on Orlo. "Why you?" he asked.

"Why me?"

"Orlo, once you moved the body, you weren't that useful. Purlew didn't really need your help. But he wouldn't let you leave. Why'd he keep you around?"

"Yeah, I wondered. At first, when he was practicin' on the animals I brought 'im," said Orlo. "I figured, hell, the guy wants a little company. I'm the only friend he's got, right? But then, while he was working over Elvira, he kept sayin' 'Watch. See how I do this. Pay attention.' And then he goes, 'I want you to do me just like this.'"

"To do him?" asked Otis.

"Wow. He wanted to be a mummy?" asked Natalie.

"Jesus Christ," said Maury.

Orlo nodded.

"And the reason he picked you," said Otis, "was your experience stuffing animals."

"I guess so," said Orlo.

After a moment of silence, Otis said, "Is she out there?"

"Who?" said Maury. "Out where?"

Orlo knew what Otis meant. "Elvira?"

"In the pyramid?"

"I guess."

"What do you mean, you guess?"

"I never came back t'help Frank, after we wrapped up Elvira." He shook his head. "I couldn't face another night in the dark here with those empty eye sockets starin' up at me."

I can understand that," said Otis.

"Daddy," said Natalie. "We have to open the tomb!"

"The tomb?" said Carol.

"I know. We have to," said Otis. "But we'll need more help."

Otis climbed out of the dugout, found a spot where his phone got reception and dialed A.J.

CHAPTER 30

Pyramid Purlew's attempt at a memorial pyramid to Elvira was a modest structure in height—Jim Otis guessed it had been barely eight feet at its apex—but it was heavy. The crudely squared blocks that Purlew had laboriously stacked above his wife's burial chamber consisted of low-grade granite chipped and muscled from the rim of the Bensonville quarry. Purlew had arranged the blocks atop a platform of four-by-four timbers that had strained beneath their burden while absorbing two decades of rain and snow, freeze and thaw. The steady gnawing of wood-borers and termites had applied the last straw.

"This thing prob'ly caved in a few years ago," said A.J. "Purlew should've treated that wood before he laid it out."

Otis was hesitant to even think the words "crime scene," but since busting into the Purlew dugout, he had felt a hunch nudging up at his diaphragm.

"We need to get inside down there," he said.

"No sweat, James. With this crew, it won't take long to open up."

A.J. had brought his wife, Kiayla, who had brought a picnic, and son Jesse, who had brought Tatum. The big dog, slobbering and ecstatically leash-free, romped through weeds and woods and blueberry bushes, growling at phantom rabbits and barking at imaginary wolves.

Otis had wearied of Orlo's company. He had Maury drive him back to La Valle. Maury was back at Purlew's clearing in less than an hour to join in the excavation. This left Earl—excused from the heavy lifting with a bad back—solely in charge of law enforcement in greater Hercules.

Carol and Natalie had never left.

A.J. was right about many hands doing short work. Within twenty minutes, the crew had cleared enough of Purlew's pyramid to expose a gap in the twisted timbers large enough for a man to enter Elvira's chamber.

With the afternoon sun at an angle, no light penetrated the pit.

"Daddy, can I go?" said Natalie.

"Of course not. Nobody knows what's down there," said Otis.

"Anubis!" replied Natalie. "Osiris! Isis, Nepthys, Neith and Selqet!"

Otis, inured to his daughter's penchant for showing off, ignored this. He said, "I guess I should check it out."

"Well, I sure ain't goin' down there," said Maury.

"I don't mind," said Teddy.

"No, I'll go," insisted Otis.

"Y'know, it might be cursed," came a voice from the woods.

Tatum, alert to an intruder, bounded toward the sound, barking in bass-baritone, only to stop short and prick his ears quizzically at the sight of a human creature half his size.

"Riley?" said Carol, surprised.

"Hiya," said Riley Hawkins, patting Tatum fearlessly and pushing his bicycle toward the excavation.

"How'd you find us, Riley?" asked Carol.

"Oh, I knew about this place," said Riley. "I been all over up here."

Otis regarded Riley with a mixture of disapproval and admiration. "I'm surprised you didn't manage to break into the dugout."

Riley shrugged. "Hey, I tried, but that's a hard door," he said. "What's down there, cop?"

"Never mind," said Otis. "You can just stand there and watch."

"Sure thing, cop."

"Call him 'Chief,'" said Natalie.

Riley turned toward Natalie, looked her over and smiled rakishly. "Okay. What's your name?"

Natalie didn't respond to Riley. "Daddy, are you going down there, or should I?"

"I'll go," said Riley.

Otis waved a hand. "I'm going, I'm going."

Otis took a deep breath. He stepped gingerly on a tilted timber and lowered himself toward the opening. He had to twist his body to get through. His feet dangled for a moment, and he let go. He thumped to the floor of the chamber quicker than he'd expected. The burial room was barely six feet deep. Crouching and peering around, he tried to accustom his eyes to the darkness.

"Whaddya see?" shouted Maury.

"I don't see anything yet."

Otis was reaching for the flashlight on his belt loop when it hit.

A wind like the breath of an angry god, ice-cold and deafening in its roar, seized and tossed him like a palm frond in a hurricane. He was off his feet, clawing at the air, blind in the black pit and, suddenly, thrown headlong into a wall. His mouth gaped, but he had no breath. He felt fingers, thin and hard, brushing his lips. They entered him and touched his tongue. He snapped his teeth, biting them off, feeling them turn to bitter dust that filled his mouth. The wind grew in force, pressing at him as though its purpose was to flatten him into two dimensions, a grotesque mural of himself on a surface no one would see.

Otis had entered the domain of death. It wanted him. He

felt its desire like a hand over his face, its fingers inside his nose, its grip crushing his skull. Its voice bellowed inside his head in a language that made no sense. Its anger was like an icepick thrust into his ear.

Otis closed his eyes, despite the power that wanted them open, wanted him staring at the consuming void. Laboriously, painfully, he drew in a thread of air. He went limp against the wall. He ceased to oppose the crushing force that pinned him helpless. He steadied his breathing and drank in air. He emptied his thoughts and swallowed his fear. He waited.

Otis had no idea how much time had passed before the pressure receded and the roar fell silent. The lunatic voice trailed into silence. Otis slumped to the floor, chilled and sweaty. He ran his hands over himself, feeling for crushed ribs, torn flesh. But there was no change. He stood weakly. He heard voices.

"Daddy?"

"James, are you all right?"

"Jim, it's dark down there. Use your flashlight."

Spent by his struggle, Otis got shakily to his feet. He unhooked the flashlight on his belt and flicked it on. Its brightness dazzled him.

"How long have I been down here?" he shouted.

"How long?" came the voice of A.J. "You just got there."

"Just got here?" said Otis, confused. "A few minutes?"

"Nah. Ten seconds," replied A.J. "What the hell's goin' on with you?"

Otis' eyes adjusted. He was facing Elvira's coffin, a sarcophagus rather, hewn apparently from a single tree trunk. It was mounted on a sturdy frame of four-by-fours. The collapsed ceiling had partly buried it.

Otis answered A.J. "There was something ..."

Otis turned, scanning the space with the light. He pointed the beam at the wall opposite the sarcophagus. Above a table strewn with objects that seemed randomly chosen, the walls were painted with crudely drawn efforts at hieroglyphics, men and women, strange-headed deities, animals, especially cats, the mocking eye of Horus. Casting the light upward, Otis saw an inscription in English.

"Something?" shouted A.J. "What?"

Otis read the inscription.

"Apparently, there's a curse," he said.

"A curse?" asked A.J.

Otis heard Riley's voice. "I knew it!"

"Jim, you're not making sense," said Carol. "Are you okay?"

"Listen to this."

Otis read: *"As for anyone who enters this tomb unclean, I shall seize him by the neck like a bird. I will plunge him into the darkness of his greatest fear, where he will be judged as evil by the great god and torn asunder by the demon Ammut. So help me, Anubis!"*

"Wow!" This was Natalie. "Daddy, that's King Tut's curse! When he was buried, the priests cast a spell to keep out grave robbers."

Otis didn't want to blame King Tut's morticians or even Pyramid Purlew for his latest encounter with a primeval force within the darkness that inspires depths of fear that plunge people into their worst, weakest moments and summons the monsters that terrified them before they were old enough to perceive their demons' unreality and shrug them off. Maybe, Otis thought, Francis Purlew had toyed so long and intimately with death and dead things that he had loosed from the grave that insidious worm of horror, bearing the venom of madness, that settles in the creases of every human mind.

Maybe there was a "curse" on this tomb. Maybe, thought Otis, he had just dropped into a pocket of gas that had made him hallucinate. Either way, he stood unscathed in the burial chamber. But he was uneasy in the presence of the dead woman inside the box, wary of what might suddenly boil up from the gloom.

If there was a dead woman.

"Hey," he shouted, "we have to clear everything away. We have to open this box. We need light."

"A box?" asked Carol. "There's a box?"

"Yeah, of course," said Otis, feeling the fatigue of his struggle. "C'mon. Start digging!"

Otis directed the clearing of Purlew's pyramid, aware that a dropped block of stone could smash the sarcophagus and strew its contents all over the floor. He wanted Elvira intact.

The job took two hours. It was late afternoon, and the sun was behind the trees. But it was June. Sunlight filtered through the forest into Elvira's little tomb. Before Otis could hold her back, Natalie leapt nimbly into the chamber, weaving between pyramid blocks scattered on the floor and squinting at the inscriptions on the wall.

"I wish I could read hieroglyphics," she said. "But I don't think Pyramid Purlew could either. All this writing he did on the wall, it looks like he just copied stuff from a book. It's King Tut's curse, but he added stuff. Daddy, look here."

Natalie pointed at an arched doorway painted on the wall where Otis had been trapped by the wind of the underworld.

"The Egyptians called this a *stela*. The dead person went through there to begin the journey to the afterlife," Natalie said. "But it shouldn't be there. It should be behind that table."

She stood before the table opposite the sarcophagus, peering at the items arrayed on the table top.

"Look, there's a toaster and a blender. An eggbeater, dishes and silverware, and a coffee cup. Ooh, it's got an 'E' on it. For 'Elvira,' right? Oh, wow, ladies' clothes! A dress and a bra and panties and stockings. And her favorite shoes. You see how worn they are? She was gonna wear all this stuff, so she could look her best on her journey through the underworld. This is so cool!"

Carol had joined Natalie in the tomb.

"Nat, these were things that Elvira needed in the next life?" she asked.

"Oh, yeah! This is the offerings table. But it should be over there, in front of the doorway, the *stela*," said Natalie. "See? Here's a picture of a man. That must be Purlew. He must've wanted her to take along a picture of him."

"Love after life," said Carol.

"Love?" said Otis. "Yeah, well, we'll see about that."

He told Natalie and Carol to not touch anything. He warned the others to stay out of the tomb. "Especially you, Riley."

Otis pointed at Jesse Cartwright. "And keep that dog out of here!"

"Yes, sir."

Pyramid Purlew, hardly Rembrandt, had painted an effigy of Elvira on the coffin lid. Her face was a pallid circle in which her eyes were enormous orbs with black pupils staring upward. Purlew had depicted his wife in a black burial robe dotted with five-pointed stars, reminiscent of the Dallas Cowboys helmet logo. Her arms, as thin as broomsticks, jutted from her sleeves. Her clawlike hands lay across her bosom.

"Jeez, Daddy, she looks like the wicked witch of the West, only a lot uglier."

"I think he meant well, Nat," said Carol.

"Okay, but if I get killed," said Natalie, "don't let Daddy paint my picture."

Pyramid Purlew had hinged the sarcophagus and sealed it with a single hasp and padlock. The wood of the casket was still solid but not so firm that Otis couldn't pry the hasp screws out with his pocket knife. He fit his fingers under the lid. All he had to do was lift.

"You ready?" he said.

"Yes, yes! Open up!" said Natalie.

Otis complied. Scanning with his flashlight, he regarded the remains of a person, presumably Elvira Purlew, wrapped head to toe in strips of secondhand clothing from the Goodwill thrift store. The mummy's surface evinced a dull sheen, as though it had been lacquered after wrapping. Otis could only assume, based on Orlo's testimony, that the now-hardened preservative substance was honey.

"Jeez, Daddy, she's really small."

Otis guessed that the mummy in the box was barely five feet long. In its dried, shrunken, disemboweled and stuffed condition, it could not weigh much more than seventy pounds.

The rest of the rescue squad was lined up on the edge of the pit gazing at the mummy. "So, this is what became of Elvira," pronounced Maury.

"This is what became," responded Otis, "of whoever's under all this wrapping. This body—if there's a body in there—has not been identified."

"Yeah, well, you got a point there, Chief," said Maury.

Otis ordered Maury to get on the phone to Minnie. "There's a professor up at the university. He's an Egyptologist. Named Weinstein. Tell her to get in touch. She should tell him to get down here tomorrow morning."

"How did you know about this Weinstein?" asked Carol.

"I looked him up," said Otis.

"Wow," said Natalie. "An Egyptologist."

"I don' know, Chief," said Maury, shuffling irresolutely and sending dirt into the burial chamber. "Ya think he'll come down here, from the university?"

Maury pronounced "university" as though it were synonymous with the Vatican.

"Maury, Weinstein is a mummy guy," said Otis. "We've got a mummy."

"Oh, well, yeah, I guess."

"Maury, call Minnie!"

"Y'sir."

"All right, now, carefully," said Otis, "let's get Elvira out of this hole."

“If it is Elvira,” said Carol.

Otis shrugged and spoke into her ear. “Who else could it be?”

“This is fun!” said Natalie.

With all hands on deck and Tatum circling inquisitively, Otis’ crew moved the sarcophagus undamaged onto the bed of A.J.’s pickup. Otis ordered the mummy stored and locked inside the storage room behind the bar at A’Jay’s.

When Otis got back to the police station, Minnie said that Dr. Ambrose Weinstein, head of the Archaeology Department at the University of Wisconsin, would be arriving in Hercules at eight o’clock the next morning.

“He sounded pretty juiced, Chief.”

“Did you tell him to meet us at Calamity’s?” asked Otis.

“Where else?”

“Good girl.”

“Girl?”

CHAPTER 31

(Sunday, the 22nd of June)

The bells of St. Peter's were tolling for nine o'clock Mass when A.J. and Otis muscled Pyramid Purlew's sarcophagus from A'Jay's back room and set it down on three tables, lined up in a row, in the main barroom. Dr. Ambrose Weinstein beamed at it eagerly and spread his arms in a gesture that suggested both welcome and wonder.

Otis had expected the University of Wisconsin's foremost Egyptologist to be a tweedy septuagenarian with wire-rimmed spectacles, orthopedic shoes and a cool air of scholarly detachment. What he met that morning, bustling into Calamity's and nearly shaking Otis' hand off his arm, was a burly man of roughly forty years with a ready grin, busy eyes and a tendency toward sudden, enthusiastic movements that involved his arms. He was six-and-a-half feet tall, with a shock of black hair, horn-rimmed aviator glasses, a thick auburn beard and the body of a gone-to-flab offensive tackle. He was in blue jeans with a Hawaiian shirt that depicted hula girls and seaplanes flying over palm trees. He was wearing flip-flops.

"I can't stand to get dressed on Sunday," he said to Natalie, flirtingly. "How 'bout you, babe?"

"Oh," said Natalie, in t-shirt, shorts and sneakers, "hate it."

Weinstein insisted that everyone call him "Finx," which

went back to his infancy, when his parents, both archaeologists, had shown him a picture of the Sphinx. He had pronounced it "finx," which Mom and Dad found so cute that they hung it on him for the rest of his life.

"It beats Ambrose," he said. "So, what the hell?" He smiled gloriously at Natalie, and she smiled back. They had bonded.

Weinstein had allowed Otis to buy him a quick cup of coffee before hurrying down the street to behold the reason for the scientist from Madison's pre-dawn drive down Highway 33. Otis, Weinstein, Carol and Natalie arrived at A'Jay's just as A.J. was unlocking his bar.

By the time the sarcophagus had been positioned, ready to open, the audience had grown. Riley, of course, was there. As an overture of apology for scaring her nearly to death, Riley had brought along the girl next door, Analise Grimaldi, chaperoned by her big sister, Maddy. Analise looked nervous but brave. Crystal had got wind of the unveiling. She showed up in a hooded floor-length caftan in broad vertical stripes of fawn and indigo, cinched with a kangaroo-hide belt highlighted with Australian sapphires and etched with the strange device, "G'DAY MATE".

Among others present and keeping a respectful distance from the presiding professor were Teddy and Earl. A.J. had asked Kiayla not to come, so she did. Jesse had tagged along with his mother, and he had brought Tatum, whose nostrils were flaring almost audibly at the emanation exuded by the contents of the big, fascinating box.

Otis had asked Minnie to skip church to be present at the unveiling. He thought Minnie more likely than anyone else in Hercules to recognize the remains beneath the wrappings. Minnie had replied, "Church? Who goes to church?"

The crowd, altogether, was a dozen souls, all quiet and tingly with anticipation.

Following Weinstein's instructions, Otis and Earl removed two hinges from the sarcophagus and lifted away the entire lid. The sight of the mummy, for those tall enough to see over the edge, caused a rustle of gasps and mutterings.

After holding his face devotionally in his hands and rolling his tearful eyes, Dr. Weinstein addressed the mummy. He patted and tugged in a few places. He ran a hand over the surface, then licked his fingers.

He smiled. "Honey," he said.

"We knew that," said Natalie.

Weinstein looked around, saw the twinkle in Natalie's eyes and let loose a single guffaw. Then he plunged back into the sarcophagus.

Weinstein gripped the mummy's head gently and applied pressure left and right. "Ah," he said cryptically.

He turned toward Otis. "This is really quite well done. Skillful. Who was the, uh ... mortician?"

"Francis Purlew," said Minnie. "Folks called him 'Pyramid.'"

"Hah," said Weinstein. "That's good. And fitting. He knew what he was doing."

"Apparently," said Otis, "he practiced on animals. Roadkill, mostly."

"Well, plenty of that in Wisconsin," observed Weinstein.

"Didn't the Egyptians make mummies out of animals, too?" asked Natalie, who knew the answer.

Weinstein turned back toward Natalie, aiming his arms at her. "That's right." He looked around. "Who is this astute young woman?"

"I'm Natalie."

"She's my daughter," said Otis. "She's been studying ancient Egypt."

"She certainly has!" said Weinstein. "Would you mind assisting me, Natalie?"

Natalie was momentarily flustered. "Me?"

"Yes, you."

"Oh, well, then, yeah."

"Good, please hold this steady."

Weinstein had brought with him a wooden case. He handed it to Natalie and unlatched it. Weinstein removed a pair of bandage-cutting scissors, flourished them once and went to work on the mummy's head. He cut each strip of cloth gently and individually, clearly enjoying the process.

"I've handled my share of mummies," he said, pausing in his work, "but never one this fresh. This is quite a thrill."

After cutting a clean line from the chin to the top of the mummy's skull, Weinstein delicately pulled aside the wrappings, exposing its face. Otis leaned close. Natalie went up on her tiptoes. The crowd craned and murmured.

The mummy's jaundiced flesh had sunken to the bone, its lips retracted from its teeth, revealing a narrow, tetanic grin. Its hair was matted on its forehead. Its nose was a sharp brown beak. Otis remembered Orlo's promise to replace Elvira's eyes with the glass orbs he used when stuffing deer. But these had never been delivered. Instead, the mummy's empty sockets were hidden by two distorted staring red eyes painted on white poker chips and secured with some sort of glue.

"All right, Minnie," said Otis. "Take a look."

Fighting her way past Tatum, Minnie edged to the sarcophagus and bent toward the mummy. Intent and impassive, she gazed at it for the better part of a minute, inspiring suspense and enjoying it.

Finally, she said, "Well, Jimmy, I wouldn't know."

"Oh," said Otis, already dreading the ordeal of extracting a DNA sample and somehow finding a verifiable matching fragment of Elvira Purlew left behind in the Kuckuck building.

"Except," added Minnie.

"What?" said Otis. "Except what?"

"Well, you know, Elvira did all her food shopping at Shutter's," said Minnie.

"I knew that," said Otis. He remembered hearing that tidbit from Maisie Hopkins. "So what?"

"Well, I remember once I was behind Elvira in the line at

Shutter's. Marie Dupee was the cashier there, sweet old biddy but slow as molasses. So I ended up staring for ten minutes at the back of that woman's neck. I couldn't help but notice that she had a mole there, I swear, bigger than a Lincoln penny."

"Who had a mole? Marie?" asked Hap, who never missed a local sensation.

Minnie turned on Hap with a scathing look.

"Elvira," she said. "Elvira had a mole."

"On the back of her neck?" asked Hap, pointlessly.

"Yes."

"Dr. Weinstein?" said Otis.

"Call me Finx."

"Okay, Finx, I have to ask. Did the Egyptians remove moles from their mummies?"

"Good question," replied Weinstein. "Nobody knows for sure."

"Would Purlew know either way?"

"No, he wouldn't," piped Natalie. "I never read anything about moles."

"Natalie's right," said Weinstein, beaming again at the girl. "There's nothing written in the *Book of the Dead* about skin blemishes."

"Well then, Finx," said Otis, "why don't we turn her over and look at her neck?"

"Oh, love to," said Weinstein, rubbing his hands together. "But first, let's get this body out of the box."

Minnie backed away. Natalie, holding Weinstein's equipment box reverently, made room. Otis enlisted Earl, A.J. and Teddy to help him lift the mummy clear of the sarcophagus. Hap Schaller emerged from the crowd and directed three other men to help him set aside the ungainly casket. Kiayla deftly laid two tables with tablecloths. Tatum whined and snuffled at the flood of sensation that assailed his senses.

Visibly atremble with excitement. Weinstein went to work on the mummy. In another twenty minutes, he had lovingly unwrapped the mummy's entire head. He directed Otis and Teddy to lift the body high enough off the table to expose the cervical spine.

Minnie sucked in her breath. She crouched and peered up at the mummy's neck.

"Dear Lord, it's her. Elvira," she said.

A burst of OMG exclamation swept the room. Natalie uttered a squeal of archaeological triumph. Tatum executed a puppy wriggle and howled rumblingly. Several people, uncertain of how to respond to this sort of revelation, executed high-fives. Throughout this macabre celebration, Weinstein instructed Otis and Teddy to hold the mummy's position exactly in place. His exuberance had waned. He appeared perturbed.

"What is it, Finx?" asked Otis when the room had quieted.

"I don't quite know, but there's something out of joint here," said Weinstein. "Lower her down, very carefully."

Otis and Teddy followed orders. Weinstein studied the mummy, cautiously manipulating the head. He let her go and dug into his case, removing a scalpel. With it, he cut an incision through the stiff wrappings from Elvira's chin almost to her sternum. He spread the crumbly fabric open. He leaned forward 'til his nose was almost touching Elvira's. Gripping the scalpel, he cut into her skin, opening her neck and spreading the brittle tissue. He gazed inside the mummy.

Weinstein hovered motionless for a long moment, his eyes first focused at the body, then blank and unseeing. Finally, he stood straight, towering over everyone. His eyes unglazed and he looked at Otis.

"Chief," he said, "this woman was murdered."

"Jesus H. Christ!" said Hap Schaller.

"Oh dear God," said Crystal.

Riley tugged at Natalie's t-shirt, almost spilling Weinstein's tools. "I knew it," he said. "It had t'be somethin' like that."

"Wait! Finx," said Otis, raising his voice above the hubbub, "how can you say that? How do you know?"

"The reason I did this incision," said Weinstein, pointing to the mummy's neck, "was to see if her hyoid had been broken."

"It was?"

"Yes."

"She was strangled."

"After a fashion," said Weinstein.

Everyone was listening now.

"When I felt her head, I thought something was ... amiss," said Weinstein. "Her neck was broken. But that could have happened post mortem, during the embalming. I had to make sure."

Silence reigned. Otis looked down at Elvira, her shrunken and yellowed head exposed, the rest of her shrouded in rags and flakes of hardened honey.

"Whoever killed this woman attacked her so violently, while he was choking her to death, that he broke her neck," said Weinstein, obviously struggling to stifle his exhilaration over this discovery. "This was an act of mayhem."

"Oh God," said Minnie. "Poor lonesome Elvira."

"I wonder who could have done this?" asked Weinstein.

"Oh, I think we have a good idea," offered Carol.

"You do?" asked Weinstein. "This woman's been dead for at least twenty years. How could you possibly—"

"Well, Finx, I believe we have a witness," said Otis, coolly.

"Who?"

"If my guess is right," Otis began. He broke off and changed the subject.

"Finx," said Otis, "I don't know as much about mummies as my daughter, but isn't it true that they can deteriorate real fast once they're exposed to the air?"

"You're right, Daddy," said Natalie.

Weinstein nodded agreement and squeezed Natalie's shoulder.

Otis turned to Minnie, who read his mind.

"I'll call Digger," she said

"Our situation is that we dug up a mummy, which was weird, but sort of fun," said Otis.

"Oh, Daddy, it was a *lot* of fun."

"But now, thanks to you, Dr. Weinstein," Otis went on, "we have a murder victim, which is serious. We need to get this body on ice."

Minnie waved her phone and announced that Ron Cedarfield, the town's Protestant undertaker, besides being chairman of the city council, was on his way. Cedarfield's funeral home had cold storage for a half-dozen corpses.

"A murder?" said Teddy to no one in particular. "Holy shit."

"Copy that," muttered Earl.

CHAPTER 32

Ever since the humans had pried open that big box, Tatum's delicate olfactory system had been assailed by aromas unlike anything he had ever inhaled. His head swam with strange sensations, and his body quivered with desire.

The crowd inside A'Jay's surrounded that weird, alluring thing which, to Tatum's limited eyesight and absent imagination, seemed to be an immense cigar. He wove back and forth behind the humans blocking his way. Between bodies, he glimpsed a face on the thing. Was this a human? Impossible! Humans often lay down and stayed very still, but if you stuck your nose into his face, or planted your front feet onto her torso, the human would awake, sit up, splutter at you and shout to "Get off! Get down, you stupid mutt!"

Or, he would get petted.

Either way, it was always fun. But this thing in the box—which seemed to resemble a human—didn't react when bothered. It didn't sit up and shout, even though the real humans were picking it up, setting it down, poking, prodding and, in Tatum's view, playing with it—especially the big man wearing big glasses. The more this huge human played with the thing in the box, the more seductive odors filled the room and flooded Tatum's tingling senses.

He caught whiffs of bone—he loved bones—and a hint of something like beef jerky, all blended together with the smells of sweet honey, bitter dust, salt, oil and the faint, tempting aroma of dead flesh gone sour.

With all his being, Tatum ached to force himself between people, muscle them aside and get close to that weird, wonderful thing that was crooning to Tatum a Siren song of delectable aroma. But, large though he appeared, he was a gentle, cooperative dog. He held himself back all the while the giant with the glasses was busy with the thing, picking and peeling and talking to the other humans.

Tatum was a little more than a year old, a giant puppy really, within whose psyche raged a constant battle between his primordial, vulpine appetites and his two months of obedience training. Tatum's agonizing effort to restrain his appetites and to resist the overwhelming curiosity incited by the remarkable thing was a triumph of human domestication over the law of the jungle.

But then, another man arrived, emanating ever so subtly the fungal fragrance of formaldehyde. Tatum listened as this new human talked with the man who always seemed to be master of all the others.

"Hello, Digger."

"Chief, what the hell?"

"It's Elvira Purlew. Pyramid—I mean, Francis Purlew—mummified her."

"Who? Did what?"

"Digger, you're looking at the mummy of Elvira Purlew."

"Holy smokes, Jim."

"He did a pretty good job, too." This comment came from the big man with glasses.

"Digger, this is Dr. Weinstein, from the university."

"Oh, hello."

"Call me Finx."

"Finx?"

"Ron here, Mr. Cedarfield, is one of our funeral directors."

"Aha! So, you'll be the man with the icebox."

"Digger, Dr. Wein—Finx, thinks ... well, he's sure that Elvira was murdered."

"Oh my God, really? Who by?"

"No way to tell, for sure. Yet. But I'm gonna try to find out."

"Well, that's your job, Chief."

"Right, and your job is to preserve this body. It hasn't been exposed to the air for twenty-some years. We need your help."

"Of course. Glad to help. I'll get the stretcher."

Tatum watched raptly as the formaldehyde-smelling man left the bar and returned in a moment with a metal platform—which had no odor at all—on wheels. Tatum's excitement mounted as the humans lifted the thing and placed it on the platform. The formaldehyde-smelling man then wheeled the loaded platform outside, maneuvering it deftly through the doors.

Tatum was hot on his heels.

The entire crowd of humans poured out of A'Jay's. More humans joined them, surrounding the thing on the platform and making breathy human noises. As the formaldehyde-smelling man reached for a lever on the platform, others stepped aside. The legs of the platform began to fold upward, and Tatum saw his opening.

Tatum could only be a "good dog"—whatever that meant—for so long. He couldn't fight his canine imperative for another second.

Tatum rose on his hind legs and lunged.

Before anyone knew what the Great Dane was up to, Tatum's front paws landed on Elvira Purlew's mummified bosom. The dog's weight and the stretcher's imbalance triggered a cataclysm. Elvira tipped violently and departed the funeral-home stretcher, attaining altitude. She flew over Tatum's head in a plume of dust and desiccated fabric. She landed with a muffled thump on Main Street. Before anyone could reach out and seize Tatum by his collar, he had pounced on the mummy. He clamped Elvira in his jaws, rocking her up and down while he spun in circles and wagged his tail ecstatically. For a moment, the big, delirious puppy disappeared from view inside a maelstrom of rent tombwear. Shreds of Goodwill Store rags danced in the June breeze.

"Jesus Christ!" shouted Maury.

"Wow," said Riley.

"Goddammit, Tatum!" roared A.J.

Intoxicated by mummy miasma, Tatum was deaf to human intervention. He had his prize and he was loath to let it go. Outside the honeyed swirl of the mummy's wrappings, Tatum sensed the threat of capture. Tightening his jaws and tasting the psychedelic flavor of Elvira Purlew, he took off down the middle of Main Street on Sunday morning.

Yearning with all his heart to be alone with this pungent mysterious thing, to roll luxuriantly in its melange of stench and fragrance, Tatum bounded eastward, barely feeling his paws on the pavement, eyes peeled for a dark and quiet place where he could be alone with Elvira.

"Oh, my dear God," said Crystal, as she watched Tatum, the mummy flopping in his jaws, pass the police station.

"Goddammit, Jesse!" said A.J. to his son. "Why didn't you—"

"Don't you blame your son for this, this ... awful mess," Kiayla broke in. "You're the one who brought a mummy to your bar!"

Natalie grabbed her father. "Daddy, we have to catch him. We have to save Elvira."

"Oh, Christ," muttered Otis.

He started after Tatum, who had a one-block lead. Others, among them Maury, Teddy and Ron, joined the chase. They closed the gap slightly when Tatum stopped in front of Mose Irons' barber shop to seesaw the mummy in his jaws. He did this so vigorously that one of Elvira's legs separated at the knee. Her fibula described a graceful arc and landed on a manhole.

Hearing footsteps, Tatum bolted again.

"Shit," said Otis. He stopped and took out his phone.

"Daddy, he's getting away!"

"Patience, kid."

Otis dialed. Earl answered.

"Where are you, Earl?"

"Up at the middle school. Someone broke a window here. I was—"

"Get in the car now!"

"Okay, what—"

"If you can get to the corner of Main and Madison fast enough, you can stop him."

"Stop who?"

"A dog."

"A dog?"

"With a mummy in his mouth."

"A what? In his what?"

"Get going! Stop the goddamn dog!"

Otis hung up.

"Good idea, Dad."

"Thanks, kid."

Otis resumed the chase. Tatum was now leading by a block and a half, heading out of town unless Earl could intercept him. If Tatum reached the woods and fields that took over the landscape beyond Madison Street, the mummy would become a needle in a haystack.

Mose Irons' barber shop was closed on Sunday. But he was inside, waxing the floor, when he heard the hubbub and saw Jesse Cartwright's Great Dane galumphing up Main with what looked vaguely like a dead body in his mouth. This was interesting.

When Mose stepped outdoors, he found on the sidewalk what looked like a hand. He picked it up. It was definitely a hand, but an old one, its yellowed skin sunken fleshless to the bone and smelling faintly of honey. Seconds later, a bunch of people ran past, waving their arms, pointlessly shouting the dog's name.

"Curiouser and curiouser," said Mose as he spotted another object.

When he examined it, he decided that it was the forearm that went with the hand.

Mose went back into his shop for a plastic garbage bag. He dropped the hand and forearm into it and then headed back to Main Street. He followed the crowd following the dog, picking up pieces along the way of what he figured was probably Elvira Purlew. When he found Elvira's head in the gutter in front of Grace Lutheran, he knew he had guessed right.

"Hello, Elvira," he said tenderly. "Long time since, sweetheart."

Breathing hard, Otis skidded to a halt at the sight of Earl, at the corner of Main and Madison. Earl was losing to Tatum a tug-of-war with Elvira's headless mummy.

"Nice work, Earl."

"Help," replied Earl.

CHAPTER 33

(Monday, the 23rd of June)

With Teddy riding shotgun, Otis arrived at Orlo Bewick's compound not long after sunrise. Neither Orlo nor Dog was evident. Otis banged on the door 'til he heard the dog barking reluctantly and Orlo's feet shuffling even more reluctantly.

Orlo, squinting sleepily, opened the door a crack.

"Orlo," said Otis, "have you got coffee?"

"Not yet, no."

"Make some. And let us inside."

Orlo opened the door and clumped toward his kitchen. He was wearing only a long-sleeved thermal undershirt and a pair of sagging Jockey shorts. Mumbling disgruntledly, he clattered a percolator into action on the gas stove and slumped into one of his two kitchen chairs. Otis occupied the other chair, leaving Teddy to sit on a beer crate.

Orlo's ancient kitchen table was so battered that its formica was curling up at the edges. Cluttered on its surface was an array of mismatched mugs, each containing a puddle of coagulating coffee and a small fleet of cigarette butts. A jar of peach preserves, half-full, contained Orlo's only evident item of silverware, a jam-crusted buckhorn steak knife. Hardened crusts, discarded twist ties, Twinkies wrappers, a mold-blued half-doughnut and more cigarette butts augmented the tabletop still life. A dozen or so dead flies and ill-fated ants had been trapped in the smear of grime and stickum that coated the once-red expanse of faded formica. Otis was careful to keep his elbows off the table.

Shakily, Orlo relit half of a cigarette. Listening to the percolator, Otis decided against risking Orlo's coffee. Orlo rose from his chair to check the state of the coffee pot and began to grope through the chaos of his kitchen sink for cups.

"Skip the coffee, Orlo," said Otis. "Sit down. I need some answers."

Orlo shrugged, rearranged his shorts and resumed his seat.

"Where's the schoolteacher?" he said. "I liked her."

"She's busy."

"Who's the kid?" Orlo asked, nodding his head toward Teddy.

"Never mind, Orlo," said Otis. "Do you understand what it means to be an accessory to murder?"

Orlo suddenly attained an erect sitting position. "What th'fuck?"

Otis leaned in Orlo's direction. "Orlo, you already confessed to helping your friend Frank Purlew dispose of his wife's body."

"Shit," replied Orlo. "Frank was no friend."

Shaking his head, as though to clear the cobwebs, Orlo stood, grabbed one of the mugs from the table, dumped his contents onto the stack of dirty dishes in the sink and poured coffee into it. He drank off half the hot coffee in a single gulp and proceeded to cough for half a minute.

Otis waited for this performance to end. Clutching the mug, Orlo collapsed into his chair. Otis resumed, "I don't believe that's the whole story."

Orlo scowled, "Whaddya mean, cop?"

"Call him Chief Otis," Teddy interjected.

Orlo turned and spat his words at Teddy. "Who the fuck're you?"

Otis could feel Orlo's fear. "I mean," he said calmly, "that you were there, upstairs, when Frank murdered Elvira."

"Huh, whut?"

"You saw Frank kill his wife," said Otis evenly. "Did you help?"

"Aw, Jeez Christ," growled Orlo. "Help 'im? Shit, no! I mean ..."

Orlo gulped more coffee and had another coughing fit. Otis caught Teddy's eye, ensuring his young deputy's silence. He fixed Orlo in an ice-cold gaze and waited.

"Awright, awright, listen," said Orlo after a minute of coughing, hawking and spitting. He took a last drag on the cigarette. "I didn' do nothin'. She was dead when I got there. I said to him, 'Jesus Christ, Frank, what the fuck've ya done. I mean. Jesus Christ!'"

"Okay," said Otis. "You're saying you weren't involved in Elvira's death, right?"

"Goddamn right!"

"Did you know, could you tell," said Otis, "how she died?"

"Well, yeah. Frank killed her. He said so. He said, 'Goddamn the bitch, I had to.'"

Otis let this admission stand without comment.

Orlo was rolling now, eager to absolve himself. "Look, it was the middle of the fuckin' night. Midnight, one in the morning. He calls and says he needs help. I say to him, 'C'mon, Frank. You know what time it is?' And he yells, 'Get over here now, or I'm gonna come gitcha.' So, I go, awright. I come upstairs there and walk in, and there she is, laid out on the fuckin' kitchen table. Like I toldja b'fore, he's got her cut open from her hips to her armpit and he's stuffin' her guts into these big damn jars full of alcohol, or somethin' ..."

"Formaldehyde, probably," said Teddy.

Orlo glared at Teddy. "Yeah, right, kid."

He turned back to Otis, who had held his peace. "So, I say to Frank, 'What the hell're ya doin'?' And he goes, cool as a goddamn cucumber, 'I am preparing my Elvira for the afterlife,' and I go, 'Wait a minute, Frank, Elvira's *dead*. What the hell happened here?'"

"What did happen?" Otis said, finally.

"Awright, so, at first, he wouldn't say, just went on'n on about preserving Elvira's 'mott,' whatever the hell he meant by that. And I go, 'Look, Frank, I'm outa here.' I didn't want nothin' t'do with no dead body that I didn't find next to the fuckin' highway. So, finally, Frank stops what he's doin'. I mean, he stands there over Elvira, and he's got her goddamn liver in his hands, drippin' on the floor, and he says, 'I couldn't let her go.' And I say, 'Go where?' And Frank says, 'She was leavin' me. Leavin' me for good.' Well, I don' know if you know it, but Elvira had walked out on Frank before, lotsa times. Couldn't stand him. But she always came back, God knows why. Y'know, but by this time, she was sick. She had a pretty bad ticker. She coulda gone any minute, and she told Frank, 'That's it. I'm not dyin' here, not with you, not in this dump, not so you can turn me into a mummy!' 'Cause, y'see, she knew what Frank was plannin' t'do to 'er."

"Frank was waiting for her to die?" said Otis.

"Yeah, so he could make a mummy out of her."

"And she disapproved."

"Yeah, right. Disapproved," said Orlo. "And she said to 'im, you ain't doin' that to me. Said she was movin' back t'Mankato with her sister, and she wasn't comin' back, ever. Well, shit, you can imagine how Frank took *that* fuckin' news. I mean, he had a dyin' wife, ready to cash in any minute, and she's all packed up an' on her way t'Minnesota, and Frank's big dream was goin' with her. No wife. No death. No fresh body. No fuckin' mummy."

"So, he killed her?" asked Teddy, meekly.

"Oh, Jesus, kid, from what Frank told me, he jist went apeshit. Grabbed Elvira by her skinny old neck and he wrung her like a chicken behind the henhouse. I mean, I looked at her and Jesus! He jist about twisted her head clean off her neck. And Frank, he says he's sorry. Tells me he didn't mean t'kill her. But there she was, dead. And Frank still had his crazy, fuckin' dream. And he fin'ly had his body. So, there she was, still warm, f'Chrissake, and he starts workin' on Elvira. And he calls me up, 'cause he needs help haulin' her away."

"And you helped him," said Otis.

"Well, yeah."

"And you put her in your locker plant."

"Well, y'see," said Orlo, "Frank killin' Elvira, it was ... um ... spur of the moment. Her tomb wasn't ready. So, we had t'put 'er in cold storage 'til, well ..."

Orlo trailed off, sighing with relief.

"You could've told the police," suggested Otis.

"Told the police? After I helped him hide those jars full of Elvira's guts? After I helped him move the body? And freeze Elvira? After I watched 'im do all that mummy shit? Hell, I was in as much trouble as Frank. Besides, Chief ..." Orlo paused. "I never met a cop I could trust."

Otis leaned back. Orlo lit another cigarette butt. Dog, who had been lying beneath the table, kicked his feet in pursuit of an imaginary rabbit. Teddy shifted from one uncomfortable position on the beer crate to another.

Otis noticed that something else was on Orlo's mind. He said, "Did you help Frank ... bury Elvira?"

"Nope, no way," said Orlo. "He said I didn't have to help 'im finish with the whole mummy bus'ness if I promised 'im one thing."

"What was that?"

"Well, y'see, the reason I had to watch 'im work over Elvira was he wanted me t'do the same thing with 'im."

"Wait," Teddy broke in. "Pyramid Purlew wanted you to mummify him?"

Orlo nodded grimly. "Yeah," he said. "Made me promise."

Otis and Teddy studied Orlo's face, which revealed nothing but a deep weariness.

Finally, softly, he admitted. "But I didn't."

Otis stayed silent.

"I couldn't," said Orlo. "I didn't remember hardly any of what Frank did. I mean, stuffin' her guts into the jars, and sucking her brains out of her head—yeah, well, that was hard t'forget. But all those chemicals and wrappin' her up and the stuff he said, the prayers over the body, well, Jesus, how could I remember that shit?"

"So, what happened?" asked Teddy.

"To Frank?"

"Yes, Orlo, we're curious," said Otis. "If he's still alive, he's a fugitive. He murdered his wife."

"Oh no, Frank's dead," said Orlo matter-of-factly. "After he got done with his pyramid'n all, he sort of lost his will t'live. I still went up there now'n then, t'check on 'im, and then one day, he was gone. Dead, I mean. I found 'im layin' on his cot in that dark dugout shithole in the ground. The body was still warm. If I'd got there before, he could've, I could've ... Well, Jesus, talk about sad and lonely. Y'know?"

Teddy had an observation. "You could have kept your promise. He was still, um ... fresh. Right?"

"Nah, didn't know how. I toldja, I forgot," said Orlo. "So, I did the next best thing."

"You buried him?" asked Teddy. "Where?"

"No," said Orlo. "I stuffed 'im."

Otis sat up. "You did what?"

"Stuffed 'im," said Orlo. "I never thought I'd have a chance t'stuff a person. But there was Frank, dead as a doornail, fresh as a daisy. Nobody but me knew he was dead. So I gutted 'im, hung 'im and bled 'im out. And then, I stuffed 'im."

Otis and Teddy stared at Orlo, whose smile suggested an air of artistic pride.

"Wanna see?"

Otis swallowed hard. "See?"

"Yeah, he's in my gallery."

"Gallery?"

Orlo stood and gestured toward a locked door on the far side of the room. "Yeah, used t'be the garage when this was a filling station. After I moved here, I made it into my ah-tell-yay. That's a French word."

Before showing Otis and Teddy into his gallery, Orlo put on pants and a moth-eaten sweater.

The door creaked as they entered the ex-garage. Orlo flipped on a bank of fluorescent lights. Otis and Teddy found themselves in a menagerie of lovingly preserved roadkill. All around were stuffed deer—does, several tragic fawns still with their spots, bucks with racks ranging from four to twelve points, even one whose antlers were still in ragged and rotting velvet. Around their feet were raccoons, squirrels, rabbits, opossums, several house cats and farm dogs and a wild pig. A coyote bared its teeth atop a pedestal. A black bear cub with a missing arm reached out menacingly from one corner of Orlo's gallery with its one good paw. An incongruously mixed flock of decrepit crows, pigeons, ducks and Canada geese hung on wires from the ceiling. A row of chipmunks, rats, skunks and small birds—many of them partly ravaged by live rodents—occupied a shelf mounted along one wall.

"Jesus," whispered Teddy.

"Beautiful, huh?" prompted Orlo.

"Um ..."

"Over there," said Orlo, hitting a switch on the wall. A sun lamp rigged as a spotlight lit a far corner where, mounted on a plywood platform painted matte black, was Francis Purlew, posed stiffly, holding out, on one gnarled hand, a mock-Egyptian ankh amulet on a slim chain. Orlo had dressed Frank in what was probably his only suit, a brown wool blend that had suffered visibly with at least a decade of temperature swings and insect depredations in the unheated garage. The remains of a white shirt had gone brownish yellow, and mice had nibbled his apparently tasty tie. Frank's skin had browned uniformly. His cheeks had sunk to the bone, and his lips had withdrawn macabrely from his teeth. His eyes were the oversized deer orbs that Orlo had failed to deliver to Elvira. They gaped down at Otis and Teddy, conveying a sense of paralytic terror.

"Whaddya think?" said Orlo. "My peace da r'sistance."

Otis was stumped for a response. "It's well ..."

Before visiting Orlo, Otis had decided that, because Elvira had almost certainly died in Hercules, any offenses committed against her were within his jurisdiction. So, as soon as Orlo had locked up his gallery, making it safe from art thieves, Otis arrested him.

"What for?"

"I'm not entirely sure, Orlo," said Otis. "But you are a guilty man."

"Well, I can't argue that," said Orlo. "Can I call someone t'come over and take care of my mutt?"

Otis allowed this.

CHAPTER 34

The town's newspaper, the *Hercules Observer,* had gone the way of all local media in the twenty-first century, absorbed into a regional chain of pennysavers publishing syndicated drivel. The revised *Observer* had proved unprofitable and was entirely discontinued four years before Jim Otis came to town. Hence, the most reliable news source in Hercules—for updates on the saga of Pyramid Purlew, his wife Elvira and that giant dog running down Main Street with a mummy in his jaws shedding body parts—was the end of the bar at A'Jay's, where Otis had just received a fresh pint of Fantasy Factory IPA.

Besides the usual suspects, Dr. Ambrose Weinstein had delayed his return to Madison, largely to bask in the adulation—not available at the university—of people who regarded him with respectful awe for his esoteric expertise. Among the crowd also were Mose Irons, who had gathered up the breakage of Elvira, Minnie Trout, who could hardly be kept away, and the ever-curious and underemployed FBI agent Tyrone Thrush. Crystal MacDougal, in keeping with the occasion, had managed to find a Cleopatra-style white gown, scooped low at the bosom, a layered collar necklace highlighted by a row of mock lapis lazuli lozenges, and a gold satin floor-length cape. Her tiara featured a gilt cobra poised to strike.

At the sight of Crystal's ensemble, Carol had murmured. "Oh, Crys, you'll never top this."

"Don't underestimate me, babe," Crystal had replied.

A.J. was happily dealing with the busiest Monday night in years. Surrounding the regulars, the gathering was four or five rows deep. Several among the assembly had expressed disappointment that Orlo was neither at A'Jay's nor locked up in the Hercules hoosegow.

"There wasn't really anyone Orlo could depend on to take care of his dog. So, Teddy drove him back home," Otis said to Crystal. "Besides, we couldn't charge him with anything that wouldn't get me laughed out of court."

"But wasn't Orlo involved in the whole thing? Didn't he help, um ... dispose of Elvira?" asked Hap. "Whaddya call that? Accessory after the act?"

"After the *fact*," corrected Teddy, who had just earned his degree in Law, Public Safety and Security at Southwest Tech.

"Yeah, after the fact," pressed Hap. "I mean, the woman was strangled."

"Allegedly strangled," said Teddy.

"'Legedly, shmegedly," muttered Kenny.

"True," said Mose, "but then—thanks to man's best friend—Elvira went all to pieces."

"And all the king's horses and all the king's men," said Carol, smiling poetically, "couldn't put Elvira together again."

"Indeed, that's the problem," said Weinstein. "The evidence that the poor woman was murdered, quite brutally, was so damaged that now, even if we reassemble her, no one can tell how she died."

"At least not in court," said Teddy.

"Wait, ain't it some kind of crime if you help somebody hide a dead body?" Hap persisted.

Otis silenced Hap with a look. "Look, we know that Orlo helped Purlew move Elvira's body. But we only have Orlo's word on that. If he changes his story or decides it's best not to admit anything, we have no evidence. Besides, it was twenty years ago."

"It's pointless," said Minnie. "Get off it, Hap."

"Yeah, well ..."

Carol intervened. "The fact remains that Elvira was murdered, and her husband killed her. We know that because of what Dr. Wein—what Finx found. Also, there are the jars."

"Jars? What about the jars?" asked Hap.

Carol sipped her wine and struck a teacherly pose. "As Chief Otis' daughter explained," she began, "the jars found in the attic of the Purlew apartment were canopic jars, which—we assume—Pyramid Purlew, used to preserve Elvira's organs."

Hap said, "Well, yeah. That's what I figured, too."

Weinstein broke in. "Have you opened them?"

"No," said Otis.

"Are you going to? I must be there when you do."

"We will."

"Where are they?"

"Right here," said A.J. "Under the bar."

"Oh my God!" exclaimed Weinstein, galvanized with excitement. "Can I see?"

Everyone wanted to see. A.J. enlisted the aid of his co-bartender, Ernie Olson, to lift the four heavy jars, filled with murky fluid, onto the bar. The crudely etched faces of a man, a baboon, a hawk and a dog were clear, but the contents remained cloudy and unrecognizable.

"Dear sweet Isis, this is extraordinary," said Weinstein. "Think about it! This Purlew person adapted and practiced a method of preservation that goes back six thousand years!"

"Maybe so," Otis offered. "But we really don't know what's in there."

"Yes, but if these are Elvira's organs, doesn't that prove that Purlew murdered her?" asked A.J.

"No, it just proves that she died and he cut her open."

"Yecch," said someone.

"However," said Otis, "we have a reasonable belief now that Elvira was murdered. I can take these jars up to the state crime lab, and they won't laugh me out of the building."

"Oh, can I go with you?" asked Weinstein.

"Why not?"

"Excuse me, gentlemen. May I continue?" said Carol.

"Oh," said Otis. "You were talking, weren't you?"

"She was talking," said Minnie, "until interrupted by men."

"Sorry," said Otis. "Go ahead."

"As I was saying," said Carol, "we're reasonably sure that Pyramid Purlew murdered Elvira, after which he disemboweled her body. After doing that, he was naturally afraid of being caught with either the jars or the rest of Elvira. He couldn't remove both the body and the jars on the night of the murder. This was too much to carry, and all the help he had was Orlo. So, he hid the canopic jars containing his wife's lungs, stomach, liver and intestines. He risked removing Elvira's body because she was the raw material for his mummy, and she had to be fresh. He mummified Elvira and placed her in her burial chamber without her missing parts. Eventually, he would have returned to the Kuckuck building for the jars because, without them, Elvira couldn't complete her trip through the underworld to the Field of Reeds. But then, while Purlew was building his pyramid, the town condemned the building and boarded it up. It became harder for him to get back inside. And then, while Purlew was figuring out how to go back upstairs and rescue the rest of Elvira, he up and died."

"Purlew's dead?" said Crystal. "Who says?"

"He's dead," said Otis.

"Oh yeah?" said A.J. "How do we know?"

"We saw him," said Teddy Gilbert.

"Saw Purlew?"

"Yes."

"Dead?"

"Yes."

"What? His grave?"

"Not exactly."

"Where?"

Teddy paused, looking to Otis.

Otis sighed. "At Orlo's. We saw him at Orlo's," he said. "Orlo found Purlew just after he died. And he disposed of the body."

"Disposed?" said Mose with a note of irony.

"What? Orlo buried Purlew?" asked Crystal. "Where?"

"Buried?" noted Mose, in the same tone.

"That's what I thought," offered Teddy.

"Buried? No," said Otis, softly. "He stuffed him."

"He *what*?"

"Stuffed him. And mounted him on a platform. In his garage."

This revelation noisily agitated the crowd at the bar. Otis, reluctant to discuss Orlo's solution to the deceased Purlew, allowed Teddy to describe the scene.

As Teddy spoke, Otis' phone sprang to life. He looked at the display.

"Oh, Christ, another precinct heard from."

Natalie, who had reluctantly taken the morning bus back to Chicago, came on the line and listened in. When Teddy finished by revealing that Orlo had fitted Purlew with a pair of glass eyes customarily used for trophy deer heads typically hung on the walls of man caves and barrooms, Natalie said, "That is *so* cool!"

Delighted to hear from Natalie again, Weinstein said, "Young lady, I didn't have a chance to talk with you yesterday. But I want you in Madison this fall to talk to my students about your role in this remarkable incident. Would you agree?"

Natalie was quiet. Finally, timorously, she said, "Me. Talk to college students?"

"You know more than they do, kid," said Otis.

"You do," said Weinstein.

"Well, I guess."

Natalie had an afterthought.

"What about the curse?" she asked. "Do you want me to talk about that?"

"Oh, the curse! Of course," said Weinstein. "That would be fascinating."

"No. Please," Otis snapped, "don't start talking about curses."

Natalie snapped back. "But you have to, Daddy. They came after you."

Weinstein's ears perked, almost visibly. "Who came after you?" he asked.

Otis didn't respond. Natalie did. "Pyramid Purlew didn't want anybody to find the jars upstairs. So, he put a curse on the building. And then, he cursed the burial chamber, too. And my dad got attacked in both places. It's like Ammut was out to get him."

"Natalie," began Otis.

"Sh," said someone in the crowd.

Natalie went on. "Before the curse attacked my dad, it went after a bunch of kids. I read the curse on the wall of the burial chamber. Purlew copied King Tut's curse, but he added stuff. It was a worse curse than Tut's. Anybody who tried to get inside, if you trespassed, you'd be struck by whatever you're most afraid of in your whole life. It was like your own private boogeyman. Isn't that right, Daddy?"

Otis sighed.

"My dad had to fight it off. Right, Daddy?"

"Fascinating," said Weinstein. "Is this true? Did you really come face-to-face with the boogeyman?"

"Big fuckin' deal," said Kenny. "I do that every day."

Otis swallowed hard. "Look, I can't explain it. I can't really describe it. I'm not sure I believe it ever happened."

"Like a dream?" suggested Carol.

"Like a nightmare," said Crystal.

Weinstein said, "This tracks with some of my research. The

Egyptians, of course, believed in magic as much as any other civilization. There's very little record of these superstitions. Fears and spirits and superstitions like this all tend to be part of an oral tradition, like Homer's Iliad and the birth of the blues. They live on for centuries, but nothing's written down. But it's only logical that the Egyptians had an elaborate liturgy of spells, curses, charms, hexes—especially because they needed supernatural forces to protect their dead kings in the afterlife. What you experienced might have been a curse, Chief, or maybe just a bad case of autosuggestion."

"Or both," said Carol.

"Yeah!" shouted Natalie.

"After all, it's human nature," said Weinstein. "Every time you enter a dark and unknown place, you turn back into a little boy afraid of the monsters under the bed."

This got a murmur of agreement from Weinstein's audience. He raised his glass and took a bow.

"Well, James," A.J. broke in as he delivered Otis' second pint, "congratulations."

"For what?"

"Hey, you solved a murder, Chief," said Teddy.

Otis waved this off. "A murder that nobody knew about, that I stumbled into twenty years after it was committed. A murder without a murderer. There's nobody to arrest."

"It's still a murder, Fosdick, and you solved it," said Carol. "Thanks to you, this one's off the books."

"It was never on the books," said Otis, grumpily. "And the real murders, the ones that are on the goddamn books, they're still ..."

A.J. filled the blank. "There it is again, James. A bad case of the Josie blues. You're a frustrated man."

"Shouldn't I be?" Otis growled.

"Look on the bright side, James."

"What bright side?"

"I'm the bright side," said Carol, cupping Otis' face and planting a kiss.

The crowd laughed, clapped and cheered. Otis blushed.

Natalie spoke, "Oh, c'mon, you guys. I can see what you're doin'. Get a room!"

CHAPTER 35

(Friday, the 11th of July)

School had been out for more than a month. Hercules High had graduated another class. Men's and women's softball leagues had begun their seasons at Memorial Park. A fair percentage of Hercules' population had absconded for frantic family leisure at Disney World, Wisconsin Dells, a cruise ship bound for Aruba, Baja, Barbados or Tongass, or—more economically—the mosquito-infested grounds of Jellystone Park in the wilds of Warrens.

Some of those who'd stayed in town were gathering outside the Kuckuck building. A half-block of Main Street had been reduced, by the placement of aluminum barricades, to a single traffic lane, regulated by Earl, wielding a portable stop sign. Parked in front of the building were the Department of Public Works' bulldozer and an excavator, mounted with immense steel jaws that gave it the aspect of a meat-eating dinosaur, that had been rented from a construction firm in La Crosse.

To witness the demolition of the condemned and now renowned structure, there were forty or fifty gapers on hand. Among the crowd was Riley Hawkins and his possible girlfriend, Analise Grimaldi, who had regained the power of speech and recovered her personality. A dozen other kids, including the ones Riley had lured into the building, were lined up along the barriers, eagerly awaiting the destruction to come.

Police Chief Jim Otis was nominally in charge of the operation, which had been authorized by the city council. To pay for the obliteration of what had become the town's foremost headache, the council had raided the budget for new Christmas decorations. The vote had been 4–1, with Sandra Rendell opposed. She had been fighting for new Main Street holiday trimmings since she was elected. She had convinced her council colleagues that the old decorations, well into their second decade of decking the halls, were both decrepit and shamefully out of fashion. The council, however, feared the prospect that a steady flow of curiosity seekers would trespass the site of Elvira Purlew's violent demise, resulting in some sort of injury, for which the town would be liable. Hence, Sandy's holiday spruce-up was again postponed.

Otis noted the presence among the onlookers of Orlo and his dog. Tatum, keenly aware of his fellow canine's presence, strained at his leash, dragging Jesse Cartwright toward Dog. Orlo's pet, lying on the pavement and drooling, had no discernible interest in making Tatum's acquaintance.

City council Chairman Ron Cedarfield sidled up to Otis, greeted Carol cordially and leaned toward Otis' ear. "There are a couple of developers here, y'see?"

"Developers?"

"Yeah, Bob Stevens, the building contractor from over in La Crosse and that woman, y'see, in the brown suit with the nice legs? She's down from Madison, works for some outfit that leases a lot of commercial space."

"Yes," said Otis, casting a glance, "she does have nice legs."

"So do I," said Carol, competitively.

"I've noticed," said Otis, winking at Carol. "Digger, what do you think of Carol's legs?"

"Um ..." said Cedarfield, nonplussed.

"You had a point, Ron?" asked Carol.

"Oh, well," Cedarfield said, "I was just thinking that clearing away that Kuckuck building—it's the better part of this block. Could be a boost to the town, economically, if we can develop the space with the right tenant."

"Why don't we see if we can get it torn down first?" said Otis.

"You've gotta think ahead," said Cedarfield. "This is prime real estate."

"Not unless you can remove the curse," said Natalie, who had crept up behind the city council chairman. Natalie was out of school and had been set loose to spend far more time with her father than she'd ever been allowed before. Otis had wondered aloud why his ex-wife had relaxed her normally viselike grip on his daughter. Romance, according to Natalie, was the answer. She revealed that Marlon, "the insurance nerd," was making serious moves on Connie. The presence around the house of an inquisitive teenage girl threatened to cramp Marlon's style. Solution: Send Natalie to Hercules.

"Curse?" said Cedarfield. "What curse?"

The word *curse* had seismic implications. It drew people close, among them Crystal in purple overalls and an L.L. Bean flannel shirt, Angelina Killdeer, Teddy, Riley and Analise.

"She's right. There's a curse," said Riley.

Natalie looked around. Assuming an air of academic authority, she said, "The curse of Pyramid Purlew has never been taken back. You can't remove a curse by just tearing down an old building."

"Wait a minute?" said Angelina. "I thought we put this Ho-Chunk curse bullshit to bed."

"It's the Purlew curse, Angie. It's a family thing," said Crystal. "Poor Elvira's been buried and her crazy husband's dead, but he left his bad vibes behind. Right, Nat?"

"That's right. My dad almost got killed by the curse."

Otis intervened. "I wouldn't go that far."

"Me, too. It tried t'kill me, too. I was the first one!" said Riley. "And it went after Analise!" He nudged the girl beside him. "She still has nightmares, don'tcha?"

Rather than responding, Analise blushed and clutched her hands together.

"Maybe there's a curse, maybe not," said Angie. "But it's not Ho-Chunk. You can't blame—"

"We know that, Angie," said Crystal. "Calm down."

Angelina had never been known to calm down when asked. "And I'm not draggin' John Stormwalker out of his filthy old wickiup again. He can't scare off somebody else's bad juju."

"We don't need him," said Natalie, reclaiming the floor. "We need the book."

"Book? Well, this is new," said Carol. "What book?"

"The Egyptian prayer book," said Natalie. "Like in the movie."

"What movie?" asked Otis.

"You know, where Evelyn the librarian reads from the book and the curse goes away."

"Just a second here, kid," said Otis. "You're talking about the mummy movie? You said it was all wrong."

Natalie squared herself to her father. "Look, Daddy, pay attention. In the movie, there was this big book with a lock. Everybody wanted to get the book, 'cause it was supposed to be, like, magical. You could cast spells and summon the gods and raise the dead and all that. They called it the Book of the Dead. But the stupid book in the stupid movie wasn't the actual *Egyptian Book of the Dead*, which doesn't have a lock. Anybody can check it out of the library and read it. The magic book in the movie was just a movie thing, okay?"

"Okay, Nat. The movie was stupid. We've established that."

"Yeah, but the thing is, it wasn't *all* wrong. Y'see, Daddy, in ancient Egypt, there were priests—like Imhotep, for instance—who said prayers over the dead, and if you were dead, you needed somebody to say the prayers. Without the prayers, you were stuck. You couldn't enter the underworld and get into the canoe and paddle your way to the Field of Reeds."

"Who the hell is Imhotep?" asked Angie.

"So, Natalie," said Carol, ignoring Angie, "you think the building is still cursed?"

Natalie was emphatic. "I don't think it. I know it. And it's gonna stay cursed 'til we say the prayer."

"What prayer?" asked Crystal.

"Well, that's the thing!" said Natalie. "The prayer might be written in the book, like in the movie. But this isn't a movie."

"So, there's no book," Carol said.

"Right. So, we don't have a prayer," said Natalie.

"Okay, bottom line here," said Crystal. "Pyramid is dead, but his curse is alive and well, and living in Hercules, in that building."

"Totally," said Natalie.

"The kid's onto something," said Crystal. "Jim, you said you relived the worst fear of your whole life when you tried to go upstairs, right?"

"Did I say that?" Otis said.

"Yes, you did, Daddy. And it happened all over again in Elvira's tomb," said Natalie. "You blacked out."

"Blacked out?" said Otis. "I didn't ... I wasn't ..."

"So," continued Crystal, "what if the town sells the lot and the new owners put up an apartment building here where the Kuckuck building was, or a Seven-Eleven, or maybe a Wendy's? And everything seems to be copacetic, until ... one day, while someone's upstairs watching TV or somebody's downstairs eating a burger, the demon gods of ancient Egypt swoop down and spread terror, starting right here where we're standing. They up and scare the shit out of everybody in town.

Women scream. Cars crash. Grown men weep like babies. Children go into shock."

"And then," said Natalie, "they do it again. And again."

"The curse never goes away," said Crystal, "because nobody knows the prayer."

"Actually, when you think about it, we don't need the demon gods of ancient Egypt to do anything at all," said Carol. "The curse will still be sneaking up and scaring the pants off people."

"Right! I see what you mean, babe," said A.J.

"I don't," growled Otis.

"Oh, but you do, Fosdick. This is a small town, full of old wives and the tales they tell," said Carol, leaning close. "If people believe there's a five thousand-year-old curse on this corner, if they tell each other and tell their children and grandchildren that the evil spirit of Pyramid Purlew, who turned his murdered wife into a mummy, whose bones were scattered all over Main Street by the hound of the Baskervilles, trust me. They're going to keep that curse alive, and they're gonna cross the street whenever they pass this spot."

"The woman knows whereof she speaks," said Crystal.

"Totally," said Natalie.

"Cool," said Riley.

A sudden collision of steel and brick, followed by the sound of tinkling glass and groaning wood, shook Main Street. The crowd turned and watched the excavator as it bit a chunk out of the Kuckuck building. Tatum launched into a barking jag. A.J. held Jesse close. Dog growled sleepily. Unfathomable emotions played across the grizzled face of Orlo. Earl stopped traffic and turned to watch. A handful of gapers applauded briefly. The kids in the front row bounced on their feet and cheered.

Otis might have glimpsed the faint trail of evil spirits fleeing upward, but this was probably just his overwrought imagination. He wrapped an arm around Carol's waist, felt her warmth and exhaled.

Riley and Natalie looked around. They saw each other and executed a gratuitous high-five as the "Service" half of the rust-streaked S&Q Hardware marquee crashed to the street.

ABOUT THE AUTHOR

David Benjamin began his career as a storyteller in Mrs. Poss' second-grade class at St. Mary's School in Tomah, Wisconsin. His fictional memoir, *The Life and Times of the Last Kid Picked*, originally published by Random House, was reprinted by Last Kid Books in 2019. His Last Kid Books include his Paris memoir, *An Apartment in Paris*, two essay collections, *Almost Killed by a Train of Thought* and *Benjamin's Mess*, two short story anthologies, *The Melting Grandmother and Other Short Works* and *Christmas in a Jugular Vein* and sixteen novels, *Three's a Crowd, A Sunday Kind of Love, Summer of '68, Skulduggery in the Latin Quarter, Black Dragon, They Shot Kennedy, Fat Vinny's Forbidden Love, Witness to the Crucifixion, Choose Moose, Bistro Nights, The Voice of the Dog* and Benjamin's Jim Otis mystery series, *Jailbait, Bastard's Bluff, Woman Trouble, Dead Shot* and *Cheat*. As a journalist, Benjamin has edited newspapers, published and edited several magazines, and authored *SUMO: A Thinking Fan's Guide to Japan's National Sport*.

Since its launch in 2019, Benjamin's publishing imprint, Last Kid Books, has received more than fifty literary awards in eighteen genres from a dozen independent press organizations.

Benjamin and his wife, Junko Yoshida, have been married for ages. They live sometimes in Madison, Wis., and the rest of the time in Paris.